Praise for Rachel Carrington's
Burning Reflections

"Rachel Carrington writes a very suspenseful story with Burning Reflections. She gives the characters such real emotion and feeling that you are waiting to see what happens with each page turn. ...The love of Morgan and Evan is wonderfully written from start to finish. It was great to read their love story triumph over the evil that took place!" ~ *Literary Nymphs*

"The opening sequence of Burning Reflections sent spine tingling sensations as Morgan faces her attacker. ...Rachel Carrington has written a page-turner that I couldn't put down. I will definitely be looking for more stories by her."~ *Joyfully Reviewed*

"This is probably the best romantic suspense story I have ever had the pleasure of reading. I literally felt like I was in the story. ...Rachel Carrington finally made that happen for me. What an amazing author. She is definitely an author to compete with in this genre. I will be on the edge of my seat looking for new books from her." ~*Five Angels from Fallen Angels Reviews*

"Burning Reflections brings to light the horror of obsession and the lengths that mental illness can drive a person. ...Rachel Carrington has penned a love story full of action and intrigue that'll keep you on the edge of your seat from beginning to end." ~ *4 1/2 lips from Two Lips Reviews*

Burning Reflections

Rachel Carrington

A SAMHAIN PUBLISHING, LTD. publication.

Samhain Publishing, Ltd.
512 Forest Lake Drive
Warner Robins, GA 31093
www.samhainpublishing.com

Burning Reflections
Copyright © 2006 by Rachel Carrington
Print ISBN: 1-59998-402-4
Digital ISBN: 1-59998-373-7

Editing by Angie James
Cover by Scott Carpenter

First Samhain Publishing, Ltd. electronic publication: December 2006
First Samhain Publishing, Ltd. print publication: March 2007

Dedication

To the love of my life, the one who changed me, completes me, and gives me hope for tomorrow

Prologue

She was dead tired.

A hot bath beckoned her and she only wanted to go home. But the dinner date she'd made with friends earlier that week still loomed ahead. Damn. Forgot to cancel. She'd certainly meant to, but time had gotten away from her. Her options were limited now. If she didn't go, she'd get an earful from Tina, her friend from the post office, and then, of course, Tina's boyfriend, Chuck, would chime in. No, best to go and get it over with.

Shouldering her voluminous bag, she was halfway across the room when the lights went out. She came to a sudden stop, a tremor of trepidation catching her unaware. For a brief moment, her heart lurched before irritation crowded out the thoughts of her evening. As she calmed, she realized this was just another glitch in the electrical system of an old building. Every time it stormed, the lights went out. And she'd definitely seen a few gathering clouds on her way in from the hearing.

A slight rustle caused a shiver of fear to build in the pit of her stomach. She looked around the room, desperately trying to see through the blanket of darkness. Then, trying to shake off the nerves, she took another step forward before a thump made her stop.

She caught her breath and held it. *Don't panic. Sounds are magnified in the dark.* The self-talk did little to help the weakness stealing her limbs.

The darkness carried a hint of foreboding. Of awareness. She heard footsteps and the whisper of clothing.

And suddenly, she realized, she wasn't alone.

Instincts told her to run and, with a pounding heart, she took off toward the door. And collided immediately with a solid form. A body. A hand seized her arm. A scream bubbled in her throat, quickly silenced by a cold piece of metal pressed into her stomach. Shock curled in the pit of her abdomen.

Hot breath bathed her face.

Then she heard his voice, a low, insidious whisper. "I've been waiting for you for a long time."

Disbelief snaked its way up her spine. This wasn't happening. Panicked, she tried to look up in a futile attempt to see the face of her captor, but he clucked his tongue and held her tight, pressing her head against his chest. "You mean you don't recognize my voice?"

The words spilled into her ear, and she tried to focus on the nuances, the inflections which would give her the name of the rabid man now holding her. She did know the voice, but she refused to believe the man holding her was the one she knew. "I-I'm not sure..."

"Unfortunately, Dexter, I can't join you for dinner this evening. I have other plans," he sing-songed. "Sound familiar now, bitch?"

Oh, my God. Dexter Canfield. Her associate in the law firm and until now, an overall nice guy. "Dexter, what are you doing?"

He spun her around to slide the gun along her cheekbone. "You always turned me down. You know, a guy can only take so much rejection before he snaps."

This couldn't be happening. Dexter was a trusted co-worker, well-liked by all the members of the firm. "You're not thinking clearly," she began in the same voice she'd use for any of her clients who'd walked too close to the edge.

He gave her a little shove and the door slammed shut. "Don't. I don't want to hear your pathetic attempts to pacify me. It's too late." His voice raised an octave. "Don't you get it? It's too late." She heard the click of the lock as he secured them together.

Her palms damp, she clutched at the visitor's chair behind her, her nails biting into the soft leather. Night had fallen, thrusting the room into pitch black. Terror, cold and chilling, enveloped her and she began to shake.

How many times had she sat across the conference room table from Dexter in daily meetings? And how many times had she rejected him when he'd asked her to dinner? He couldn't have known her refusals had nothing to do with him. And everything to do with her ex-husband, Evan.

Her heart racing, she heard his footsteps. Was he pacing or coming toward her? A gurgle of panic lodged in her throat. "Dexter, you can't do this. Think of everything you'll lose if you go through with this. Just walk away. We'll just forget this ever happened."

The tread softened, and chills danced down her arms. She tried to lean back as far as the chair would allow. "Even now, she lies. Other plans, my ass." The gun made a swishing noise as he whipped it frantically in the air. "You didn't have other plans. You just didn't want me. You couldn't see yourself on a date with a man who wasn't up to your standards. Yeah, you'll

9

help me now when you wouldn't even give me the courtesy of a dinner date." He pushed the lower half of his body against her and panic intensified. What was he going to do to her? How could she escape? "I wonder if your kind offer of assistance has anything to do with the gun I hold in my hand?"

It had everything to do with the gun. Just the thought of it held her rapt attention and made Morgan's fingernails dip even further into the leather.

"Dex, please, listen to me. I have friends waiting for me. If I don't show up and they can't reach me, they'll call the police. You don't want that to happen. It's better to end it now." She spent her days in the courtroom convincing twelve people to free her clients. But she doubted her own abilities this time.

Because her own life depended on her powers of persuasion and not someone else's.

"Just shut up. You just shut up. You don't care for me." Dexter stomped his feet and Morgan held her breath. She should be able to negotiate her way out of this, but the words wouldn't come. She had no bargaining tool this time.

He brought the gun to her cheek and rubbed it against her skin. "I should just kill you now. Though, that was never my original intention." He lowered the weapon only marginally. She heard him pat the front pocket of his suit coat.

For a brief moment, hysteria took over, and Morgan found herself thinking about the Dexter she'd seen just this morning. They'd shared a laugh over coffee. Had he been planning this even then? Or had she catapulted the lunacy by refusing his dinner request once more?

Even now, she remembered what he was wearing. An expensive designer suit and polished loafers. And with the chiseled jaw and blond crew cut, he'd always given the impression of a more than capable opponent in the courtroom.

"You really should pay more attention to me now, Morgan."

She heard his voice, a whisper away from her ear and she tried to swallow, but a lump the size of a fist lodged in her throat. His shirt rustled, and a shadow slid across her face.

Dear God. He was going to touch her.

Tears stung the back of her eyes. Her day had begun so normally. Coffee and muffin at eight followed by an intense meeting with a client accused of armed robbery. Conference call with the judge which segued into a long lunch with one of the senior partners.

She'd come back to her office after a late hearing to grab some files to take home with her before heading out to join her friends for dinner. Would they really call the police? Dexter hadn't accepted her bluff.

An ominous click sent her mind racing back to the present. "You don't want to do this. So far, it's only kidnapping, but if you kill me, you know what could happen. My God, Dexter, you've spent the past three years defending criminals. You know the repercussions for your actions." The words tumbled over themselves and the tears began, not a rush of moisture down her cheeks. Just a drop now and again. Tiny dots of wetness she didn't bother to brush away. Her appearance mattered little now.

Dexter wasn't listening to her. He'd gone back to pacing.

"Dexter, I..."

"Shut up!" Morgan fell silent. "Just shut up. I never thought I'd say this, but I'm sick of hearing your voice. I might have known you'd be a whiner, someone who would plead for their life like a weak-kneed baby." He scrubbed the top of his head with his palm and his blond crew cut made the hair rasp against his skin. "No. Shooting you will be too easy."

He walked to the office door, but Morgan wasn't stupid enough to think she'd been granted a reprieve. She turned the chair and sank down onto the seat, not trusting her legs to keep her standing.

The carpet barely muffled his footsteps, and the next sound Morgan heard was the scrape of the metal rings against the iron curtain rod. The heavy drapes slid open, allowing the moon to cast a glow into the room.

"There. That's better, don't you think?" Moving away from the curtain, Dexter hitched one leg up on the bottom rung of a Queen Anne chair which matched the small sofa in the corner of Morgan's office. "You'd better hope your friends don't call the cops, Morgan. I would really hate to have to track them down. One by one. You'd hate that, too, wouldn't you?"

The promise of evil in his voice terrorized her and Morgan whispered, "Please let me go."

Silence fell for a long minute. "Why would I want to do that? You don't really think this was a spur of the moment thing, do you?" He gave a little laugh which chilled her even more. "Oh, no, Mrs. Hennessy. I've been planning this for a long, long time. So long, in fact, that sometimes, I would lie awake in bed and dream of this moment."

She knew then that there would be no convincing him to free her. She was going to die. Closing her eyes, she tried to recall peaceful images, visions that soothed and comforted her.

Evan's face came to mind. With his boyish good looks and easy charm, he'd always comforted her. And now, she couldn't even remember the reason they'd divorced. She wished he were here now. Holding her.

"You're not listening to me," Dexter reminded her. "And on that note, I think I'll give you something to remember me by." He tucked the gun into the waistband of his dress slacks and

Morgan stood. She wouldn't go down without a fight, dammit. Now that he'd put the weapon away, maybe, just maybe, she had a chance.

The glow of the moon showcased his angular features as he raised one finger. "No, no, no. No escape." His hand dipped into the front pocket of his shirt. "Do you smoke, Morgan?"

She didn't want to answer the question, but fear of hastening her demise forced her to respond. "No." Sweat dripped down between her breasts, soaking the front of her dry-clean-only silk blouse.

He flicked a tiny gold lighter and the flame, a vivid orange, mesmerized her. Horror clawed its way up from the pit of her stomach as Dexter approached her. "I've always been a big fan of fire. It's just one of the many things you don't know about me because you never cared enough to learn." He withdrew a silver flask from just inside his coat pocket. "Thirsty?" He offered her the container.

Morgan didn't know how he wanted her to respond, but as he continued to hold out the flask, she relented and lifted her shaking hand. He pressed her back, pushing her down into the chair once more.

"You'd better sit. I wouldn't want you to spill it." His voice sounded cordial, almost conversational.

The silver rim touched her lips and as she tipped the small bottle back, the heat of the whiskey burned its way down her throat. She coughed and sputtered, giving Dexter an opportunity to retrieve the flask before she dropped it.

"Excellent, excellent. Now, Morgan," he hitched one hip on the arm of the chair, "do you know what happens when fire comes in contact with alcohol?"

Her eyes widened. Dexter put his lips to the edge of the bottle and Morgan tried to push her way out of the chair. Terror

13

so intense she was nauseated gave her the strength she needed to dislodge him, but Dexter rebounded quickly, snatching a handful of her long, blonde hair.

He brought her face close to his, pressing his cheek to hers. "Oh, don't run, Morgan. You'd miss all the fun."

He took a hearty swig of the whiskey, struck the lighter and blew into the flame.

Chapter One

He'd found her.

But only after calling in the rest of the outstanding favors owed him by his old friends at the New York Police Department. Funny how they could find someone hundreds of miles away when his repetitive calls to every hospital in Raleigh had yielded him no returns. In the end, it didn't matter. Evan had located the right hospital. Now, as he strode down the polished halls, the antiseptic smell stinging his nostrils, anger burned deep in his chest.

With plenty of time to think on the airplane, he'd come to two solid conclusions.

He wasn't leaving Raleigh without his ex-wife, and the psycho who'd hurt her would live to regret it.

From the second he'd heard the news that morning, Evan's temper had spiraled out of control, but deep down inside, it masked the real problem—paralyzing fear for the woman who'd always held his heart.

When the morning broadcast had played out the horrific details of a hostage situation, Evan had been rooted to the spot, horror clenching his stomach. Morgan had gone through hell and not one damned person had called him. Not her parents, her friends in Raleigh. No one.

In the middle of shaving when the reporter's words penetrated his caffeine-neglected brain, Evan's hand had slipped. He touched the nick on his chin as a reminder. His heart had sunk with those words and suddenly, his day had taken a distinctly different turn.

His focus had shifted from his job as the town sheriff, protecting the citizens of Skyler, to protecting Morgan.

Now, he stopped at Room 322 inside Wake Forest Hospital. This was it. He didn't take the time to wonder why his palms were sweating. He tapped once on the door before he pushed it open. He swallowed hard and came forward, his footsteps soft.

Morgan lay against the stark white sheets. Her eyelids closed, her face pale. He'd never seen her looking so helpless. Wires connected to her from every angle and monitors beeped with annoying persistence.

He took in a deep, steadying breath before he spoke. "Morgan?"

Her lids flickered and her eyes, a haunting green, focused on his face. "Evan?" Her voice sounded as raspy as a dull saw rubbing metal. "What are you doing here?" She tugged the sheet higher up her neck.

He approached her, never taking his eyes off her face. "If you thought I'd stay away, you don't know me very well."

"How did you find me? The police said they were keeping my location a secret."

Evan knew her too well. She was fidgeting, her hands twisting the spotless sheet around her knuckles. "You don't really need me to answer that, do you?"

Her gaze dropped from his face. "We're divorced."

He didn't need the reminder. "It doesn't change how I feel." He stood by the side of the bed. Instincts pushed him to reach for her, but he knew she was swathed in bandages. He wasn't sure about the extent of the damage, but he recognized the morphine drip next to the side of the bed.

From what the nurse had told him, the entire left side of Morgan's body had borne the brunt of the bastard's sickness, and he saw a deep-rooted emotional pain on Morgan's face that went far deeper than any physical scars.

He hooked his foot around the chair behind him and dragged it forward to sit. "I would have come sooner."

She wouldn't look at his face, wouldn't meet his eyes. Evan felt her anxiety, her fear. It beat at him like a hunger. And when she spoke, her voice was broken, like a child's discarded toy. "You really shouldn't be here."

He edged closer to the bed. "But I am here. I want to help you." He crammed his hands into his pockets to give them something to do. "Are you in pain?"

"Not much. The medication helps."

He heard the lie in her voice. "Morgan, I want to help. Tell me what I can do." He'd never felt so helpless or useless in his life. He hated the weakness, but more than that, he hated seeing Morgan in pain. And knowing there wasn't a damned thing he could do about it.

Her eyes lifted and the stark terror he saw swirling within their depths squeezed his heart. "He's not finished."

Fury roared its ugly head, creating a need to strike out. Evan surged to his feet. He wanted to shout, to throw the chair through the window, but mostly, he wanted to find the son-of-a-bitch who'd done this. He struggled to rein in his anger and softened his voice, trying to comfort the woman he once called his wife.

"He won't hurt you again, Morgan."

She averted her face again and he thought he heard a sob. "Evan?"

"Yes, baby?"

"Could you please leave?"

Her words stunned him. "What? You expect me to leave you now? Morgan, I can't. Ask me to do anything but that."

"I have to ask." Her voice broke.

"I can protect you." He'd spent the last fifteen years of his life in law enforcement. She knew that. So why was she pushing him away?

She shook her head almost violently. "No, you can't. You have to leave. Please." She sounded almost frantic, desperate to convince him.

"Morgan, what are you saying?" He leaned closer to her, one hand resting next to her shoulder. "What is it you're not telling me?" His lips brushed her ear.

"Evan, please."

He closed his eyes, his heart aching. Couldn't she see how much he needed to help her? He couldn't walk away from her. "I'm not going anywhere. I can't leave you as a target. You need to come home." He tucked a strand of golden hair behind her ear.

"Raleigh is my home." Tears coated the words.

Evan bit back a violent curse and straightened. "You can't stay in Raleigh." He enunciated the words carefully. "The bastard knows where you live." He heard her sharp intake of breath and knew he'd caught her attention. He wondered if she'd relent now.

"I don't want to talk anymore. Evan, I can't think about this right now. I just... I don't want you here."

"Bullshit. Tell me what's really going on. Why do you want me to leave?"

Tears began to leak down her cheeks. "He'll hurt you, too."

That was it. He was going to hunt the asshole down. He still had connections at his old job with the New York Police Department. They could find a seed in a windstorm. He'd find Dexter Canfield.

And he'd kill the son-of-a-bitch himself.

Long after she'd finally convinced Evan to leave, Morgan lay awake, staring at the ceiling. She'd counted the tiles and the steps it took the nurse to get from her bed to the door. And she clutched a mirror in her hand, waiting until she could summon the courage to use it.

The same refrain rolled through her mind over and over.

The bastard had spared her face.

But as Morgan positioned the hand mirror next to her side, the knowledge didn't make her feel any better. She held her breath as she peeled the sheet back, and as she began to lift the bandages, pain sliced through her abdomen. She bit her lower lip and counted to ten while tugging on the white wrap.

Then she saw what the doctors really didn't want her to see. Angry, oozing sores. Red and puckered. Her skin looked like a jigsaw puzzle that hadn't been put together properly.

Nausea welled inside her while tears filled her eyes. For some reason, Dexter had directed the flame away from her hair and face. She tried to be thankful, but instead, she could only think about what she'd lost. Much more than just her unblemished skin. She'd lost her confidence. Her ability to face the world without panic.

The doctors said the scars on her left side would be permanent. They'd given her the usual platitudes about still having a long life ahead of her.

But seconds before she heard the sirens outside the window of her office, while she lay on the ground writhing in pain, Dexter had made her a promise. One which changed her life more than the scars.

He would come back to finish the job.

Seven weeks later

The rain beat down on the roof and glittered against the windows. With every light in her condo on, Morgan stood in the center of the living room, praying she hadn't really heard the thump.

Her nerves stretched thin, she clutched the baseball bat in both hands and held it against her shoulder with damp palms. She wasn't even sure she could use it, but her unwelcome visitor didn't know that. God, why had she insisted on coming back to her place? Why hadn't she listened to her parents and just gone home with them? Did she really need to prove she was strong enough to stay alone so soon?

She edged closer to the door on shaky legs. Her teeth chattered and fear nipped at her heels. She pressed her ear to the heavy oak just as a thump rattled the door. Dropping the bat, she shrieked, her hands covering her ears as she fell to her knees.

Her gaze swept around the room as the pounding continued. She needed her phone. Where was her phone? With tears clouding her vision, she stumbled to her knees just as a familiar voice penetrated her hysteria.

"Morgan, for God's sake, open the damned door! It's Evan!"

Relief made her muscles weak and she half-stumbled, half-lurched toward the door to wrench it open. Falling across the threshold into Evan's arms, she clung to him and sobbed.

His hands stroking her spine, he guided her back inside and kicked the door shut. "It's okay, baby. It's okay."

"No...no...no," she hiccupped. "It's not okay and it never will be again."

Evan held her tighter, pressing her against his body. Morgan absorbed his heat, his strength, glad he'd come in spite of her instructions to stay away. She'd hoped he wouldn't listen to her.

"Come on," he soothed, hooking one arm around her waist. He began to guide her down the hallway.

Morgan followed blindly. "Where are we going?"

"To pack. I'm getting you the hell out of here."

"No. I can't. I can't run from him, Evan."

He stopped and turned to cup her face. "Sweetheart, it's not running. It's recovering. There's a difference. You can't get better here all by yourself."

She sniffed and ducked her head. "My parents wanted me to come home."

"And that's exactly where I'm taking you. They're expecting you."

She shuffled along beside him, too tired to fight. "I thought you were him."

Evan cursed below his breath. "I'm sorry. I should have called first, but I didn't think you'd answer your phone."

"I don't even know where it is."

He pointed toward the foot of the queen-sized bed dominating her bedroom. "Sit. I'll pack for you."

The thought of Evan handling her lingerie sent a tingle down her spine. She wondered how she could even think about tingling when seconds ago, she'd been scared out of her mind.

Still with the same strong jaw, wind-whipped sandy brown hair, Evan made her remember him as she'd known him years ago. They'd both been no more than children when they'd met and their love blossomed from a decade spent riding bikes, swimming in the creek behind her grandparents' old house and sneaking kisses at the back of the church.

And despite the break-up of their marriage, they'd never truly gotten over one another. Some things just weren't meant to be forgotten.

"Evan?"

In the process of tugging open one of her dresser drawers, he paused, looking over his shoulder. "Yeah?"

"Thanks for coming."

He winked. "You didn't really think I would let you stay here all by yourself, did you?"

Chapter Two

Morgan stared at her reflection in the mirror, gingerly touching the ghastly scar just below her collarbone. The twisted flesh ran the length of her body from shoulder to hip and though the fire had only consumed one side of her, she felt scarred from head to toe.

"Darling." Diane Tanner spoke from the doorway and Morgan quickly tugged the turtleneck over her head to cover the grim reminders.

Diane moved into the room, catching hold of her daughter's hands. "Honey, you can't hide behind these blouses forever." She caught Morgan's gaze in the oval mirror and for a brief moment, Morgan saw her mother's pain. She wanted to comfort the woman who'd given her life, but she didn't have any words of wisdom or reassurance. She'd spent the better part of the last week since her release from the hospital trying to recover from Dexter's lunacy. And looking over her shoulder.

She'd felt safe inside the hospital. At least, as long as Evan was there. In spite of her demands, he'd stayed by her side every weekend, leaving only to fulfill his duties during the week as the sheriff of Skyler. Even then, he'd taken many days off. He'd promised he'd protect her. She'd trusted him with her heart so many years ago. How could she not trust him with her life now? And she wasn't surprised he'd insisted she come back to Skyler with him. She wouldn't have expected otherwise.

Morgan lifted her gaze to realize her mother had called her name again, trying to capture her attention. She tried to soften the moment, even managing a feeble smile. "It won't be forever, Mom. Just until my confidence returns." Which she doubted would happen anytime soon. Just the thought of stepping foot inside her old office at Baker and Snyder horrified her. Right now, she wanted nothing more than to hide and lick her wounds.

Diane sighed and placed her hands on Morgan's shoulders. "You're still a beautiful woman."

Morgan winced and moved away from the mirror, snatching her thick, wavy hair up into a haphazard ponytail. "I'm not worried about my looks, Mom."

Diane sighed audibly. "I'm sorry."

"You have nothing to apologize for." Eager to change the subject, Morgan walked to the door of her bedroom. "It's been a while since I've been here. I think I'll take a walk through the town square."

"Evan said he would stop by to see you later."

Morgan's hand stilled on the doorknob. "I'm not surprised. He thinks he's going to be able to track Dexter down. He doesn't know Dexter."

"I don't think anyone really knew that man, did they?"

Certainly not the senior partner at her old law firm. He'd practically tripped over himself assuring her Dexter had a clean criminal record. They never would have hired him had they known about his mental status.

Morgan had laughed after Mr. Snyder left. He'd only come to seek reassurance from her. He didn't want her to file a lawsuit against the firm. He needn't have worried. She didn't have the energy to fight Baker and Snyder, too.

Evan did, though. But he didn't want to fight inside a courtroom. He'd ranted and raved about the lack of security in her old office building and how he would personally kick the ass of every senior member. The thought made her smile. She didn't doubt Evan could do it.

"Morgan? Are you okay, sweetie?" Worry laced Diane's voice.

Morgan tried a subject change. "Evan told me when we left to go to New York he doubted he could stay away from Skyler for very long. He always felt a kinship for this town. While others were desperate to escape, he enjoyed the peace and quiet he found here."

"And you loved him for that," Diane reminded her in a whisper-quiet voice.

Morgan winced. "I've always loved him, Mom. Evan will always be my first love, but not all loves are meant to last. I'll be back in a little while. Don't wait dinner for me."

Diane trotted after her. "Are you sure you should go alone?"

"Weren't you the one just saying I couldn't hide forever?"

But she sure as hell wanted to.

The town square looked the same, which didn't surprise Morgan. The residents of Skyler, North Carolina didn't like change. She recognized Sam Canton's battered pickup parked in its usual spot in front of the county courthouse. Maude Elders pushed her shopping cart down the cracked sidewalk and Morgan heard the Bailey triplets, now teenage boys, exchanging lighthearted banter as they tossed a football around the small park.

For most of her life, Skyler had been home, but it didn't feel that way any longer. She'd made another life for herself in Raleigh and though her parents insisted they were proud of her, she knew they'd been hurt at her decision to leave her roots behind. Now, she wished she'd listened to them. Had she remained in Skyler, none of this would have happened.

Breathing in the deep mountain air, she kept her eyes trained on her sneakers, hoping to avoid eye contact and possible ensuing conversation with any passersby. She needn't have bothered. Once a well-loved citizen of Skyler, Morgan knew what had happened in Raleigh—what the citizens were calling a tragedy—left folks wary of how to approach her. She supposed that was a good thing.

She passed by the feed and seed store where two men she didn't recognize played a friendly game of checkers. She quickened her pace until she caught the tail end of the conversation.

"Police don't know if they'll catch the guy. Said he's some kind of a psychopath."

"I heard they thought he'd burned up in the fire."

"Nah. The only one who got hurt was Sheriff Hennessy's ex-wife. Heard tell she was hurt pretty bad. And the Dexter Canfield fella, well, he done clean escaped. Word has it he's some kind of firebug. Likes to play with the damned stuff."

"Think he'll go looking for Mrs. Hennessy?"

Panic seized her lungs, and Morgan didn't hang around to hear the response. She didn't know which way to run. She couldn't escape him. She'd never be free of him. Fear guided her and she took off toward parts unknown, running past the drugstore, careening out into traffic. She heard the squeal of tires, but she kept running. And when a voice shouted her name, she ran faster, tears streaming down her face.

Her breaths came in short gasps and several strands of her hair escaped from the confines of the scrunchie holding it back, but she had no intention of stopping now, not until she'd reached safety of some sorts.

She rounded the corner by Ed's barbershop and caught a glimpse of a tan uniform too late. She plowed into a hard chest, and the force toppled both Morgan and her unsuspecting victim to the hard concrete.

"Ooomph," came the grunt from beneath her.

Morgan struggled to right herself but a pair of vise-like arms held her in place. Familiar arms. She turned her face ever so slightly and met a pair of hazel eyes that had haunted her dreams for five years. Her sail promptly deflated. "Evan?"

His hands softened on her arms. "Yeah." His eyes searched her face. "Are you all right?"

She quickly pushed herself to her feet. "I'm fine." She brushed her hands down the front of her stiff blue jeans.

He stood beside her, but kept one hand on her arm. "You're not fine. Did you see something? You were running like the hounds of hell were on your heels."

She looked away from the concern on his face. "Funny you should mention hell," she murmured and instantly regretted her bitter words. She glanced upwards and caught the raw look of pain in Evan's eyes. She sighed. "I'm sorry. I don't mean to sound like I pity myself."

"Hey," Evan interrupted the apology. "You have every reason to pity yourself if that's what you want to do right now. You have been through hell. Now, care to tell me why you were running?"

"I just got spooked. The guys in town were talking about Dexter."

His calloused palms rubbed up and down her upper arms. "I'm sorry."

His touch reassured her, gave her strength. She didn't want to need him like this. Her teeth worried her lower lip. "I feel like I'm never going to be able to escape him."

Evan's jaw hardened. "Canfield will be caught, Morgan. He won't hurt you again." Morgan knew he was making her a promise.

She allowed herself the luxury of touching her palm to his face before dropping her hand. "I'd better get back. Mom will worry about me."

He stepped back out of her way. "I'd like to stop by and see you in the next couple of days, if that's all right."

She stuck her hands into the pockets of her jeans. "Why?"

He shrugged, merely an awkward movement of his shoulders. "Just cause."

Morgan didn't have the energy to ask any more questions. Instead, she bobbed her head and began to walk. She paused to add, "I didn't come back for protection."

Something flashed in his eyes, and she knew he wanted to protest, but he didn't. He just smiled slightly.

"I didn't," she defended. "I came because both you and my parents wouldn't stop trying to convince me that I needed to be here."

"And you always were one to do what people told you, weren't you?" he asked before turning and strolling away.

He always knew the right buttons to push.

The musty smell of mildew and the stench of garbage assailed his nostrils as Dexter carried the brown bag into the one-bedroom apartment and kicked the door shut. On such short notice, he couldn't be expected to find a room at the Hyatt. Besides, this landlord didn't ask questions.

Settling himself at the wobbly kitchen table, he dumped the contents of the grocery bag out in front of him. His hands ached with each movement of his fingers and he bit his lower lip to keep from crying out. The flesh cracked and bled, but a doctor wasn't an option. The police would suspect that.

He squeezed a healthy spurt of aloe vera cream out of the tube and slathered it on his palms. His breath hissed out of his lungs as he waited for the cooling sensation to ease. The heavy bandages came next, but even as Dexter worked, his mind sped ahead.

He'd spent the last two months waiting, giving Morgan plenty of time to heal. Sure, he'd had some fun in the process. After all, there were always people to burn. But now, he had something important to finish...or someone, rather.

"Where are you, my lovely, Ms. Hennessy? I know you survived. Such a shame to have to endure the hell a second time around." He tore off the tape with his teeth and clumsily secured the gauze wraps.

"I know I hurt you." He hummed low in his throat. "I smelled your burning flesh as I watched the fire envelop your lovely body." He shook his head and giggled. "I really hated to do that to you." He scooted away from the table and trudged into the living room area. The cracked linoleum and peeling wallpaper added to the desolation of the room. He dropped down onto the sagging sofa with his knees splayed. "I would have spared your life, but you weren't interested in me."

With much effort, he managed to withdraw the lighter from the front pocket of the chambray work shirt he'd lifted off a clothesline before he made his dash to the store. The flame flickered, providing more light than the swaying bulb overhead.

"I'm looking forward to seeing you again." He couldn't take his eyes off the mini-fire.

"Come out, come out, wherever you are," he sang quietly.

Chapter Three

Evan didn't lose sight of Morgan. He'd doubled back the second she started walking toward Elm Street. He knew she'd been spooked and the last thing she needed now was to be alone.

He followed her casually, keeping her trim body in his line of vision at all times. She'd lost a lot of weight, but he'd recognize her curves anywhere. Rounded in all the right places, Morgan's body held him captive. He'd never forgotten her. How could he? Every major trial in North Carolina brought her back into his living room. She'd been interviewed countless times on national television, showcasing her sultry beauty.

His breath came out harshly, and he realized he'd allowed the trance to distract him. He shielded his eyes from the sun and saw Morgan climbing the steps of her parents' two-story wood-frame house.

He'd wait until she was safely inside, then he'd leave.

"You might as well come up for a glass of tea," she surprised him by calling.

She'd known he was following her? Damn. "How did you know I was behind you?" He jogged toward the house now that he'd been discovered.

Morgan held open the screen door. "I've always been able to sense you."

His brain began to hum, and he reached out to touch her face, but she reacted violently, jerking her head away. His gut tightened. He wanted to kill Dexter Canfield himself, though he figured he wouldn't get the chance. The asshole was probably halfway to Canada by now, despite the threats he'd made to Morgan.

"Are you coming inside or not?" Morgan's voice held that imperious note he remembered well.

With a grin, he swept his hand wide. "Lead the way. Is Diane home?" The screen door banged shut and except for the low whir of the ceiling fans, the house oozed silence.

She tugged her hair free from the holder and threaded her fingers through its length while Evan watched the sensual movements. He doubted Morgan realized how she affected him, at least not now.

"No. Mom's at the bakery and Dad is playing golf."

Evan followed her into the kitchen. "Diane still works that bakery seven days a week."

Morgan smiled a little and started to reach overhead for the glasses. She sucked in a sharp breath and immediately lowered her arm. She turned abruptly and bumped into Evan's chest for the second time that day.

"I'm sorry. Could you please get the glasses down? I can't..." she broke off and Evan didn't require her to finish.

"Sure. In fact, why don't you sit down and let me pour the tea? I think you're supposed to be taking it easy, aren't you?"

"I'm not an invalid."

He recognized the defensive tone well. "I don't recall saying anything about your being an invalid. Just that you're here to relax and recuperate."

Morgan folded her hands in her lap. "Do you want to tell me why you were following me?"

From the corner of his eye, he saw her adjust the collar of her blouse. "Why do you think?"

"I've never needed a bodyguard, Evan."

His hands stilled on the glasses. "Maybe that isn't such a bad idea now."

"It's a terrible idea. I would never want anyone watching every move I make. It's unnerving. There are fresh lemons in the bottom drawer."

Evan squatted and tugged open the vegetable crisper inside the refrigerator. "You know," he waved a piece of the yellow fruit for emphasis, "you may want to think about it, though."

Morgan smacked the table so hard the salt and pepper shakers jumped.

He grinned and stood. "Haven't lost your temper, I see."

"My temper wasn't burned."

Adding ice to the glasses, he poured the sweet Southern tea. "Here ya go." He straddled a chair next to her and took a long swallow. "Your mother has always made the best tea in Skyler."

Morgan's gaze dropped. "I made it."

The glass halted halfway to his mouth. "Then Diane has competition." He winked, hoping to put her at ease. "Dad has already asked when you're going to see him."

Her hands clenched around her glass of tea. "I've been to enough doctors. I'll go when it's time for a check-up."

Evan reached across and touched her wrist. "He didn't mean for an office visit. You know Dad misses you."

She pulled in a shaky breath. "I haven't talked to him in years, Evan."

"He's still the same guy. He doesn't hold our divorce against you. He's smart enough to know this kind of stuff happens." He tucked a stray lock of hair behind her ear, more to feel the softness of the strand than any need to straighten her appearance. He remembered well the feel of those silky strawberry blonde tresses as they caressed his chest. The mental image created an ache between his thighs. He cleared his throat and took a hasty swallow of tea.

Morgan shifted away from the table, turning her legs toward the right, away from him. "I know a lot of people want to ask questions."

"But they won't. You should know the townsfolk better than that. They're not going to pry into your personal business."

"Will you do me a favor?"

His eyes widened. "Of course. Anything."

She reached out to cover his hand with hers, and the direct contact startled him. He wanted to turn his hand over, to capture her fingers with his, but he wouldn't risk scaring her away, not now. "Don't treat me like a piece of glass." Her fingers tightened around his knuckles just briefly before she released him. "I expect honesty from you. You always gave me that."

Evan couldn't figure out exactly where she was heading. "And I'll still give it to you, but I need to know exactly what you're looking for."

She stood abruptly and carried her glass to the sink. "I know this isn't fair of me to ask you, I mean, after the way I walked out on you..."

"Hey," he protested, "you didn't walk out on me. We both knew it was only a matter of time before one of us got tired of trying. You were just the first." He came to stand behind her and settled his hands on her shoulders. "So ask away." He pulled her slightly closer. "In case you haven't noticed, I'm here because I want to be."

She leaned back against his chest. "I don't want to let this terrify me into hiding out for the rest of my life." She turned in his arms. "Promise me you won't let me do that."

The request stunned him and for a second, he wondered if he'd heard her accurately, but then, she called his name, repeating the request.

"No." He cupped her face. "I won't let you do that. You've been through hell, Morgan, and I wish I could have been there to go through it with you. We were friends long before we were lovers. I'll always be here for you."

She gave him a wobbly smile. "Thanks. This is one time I could really use a friend."

The word didn't conjure up the exact image Evan hoped for, but it was a start. At least, Morgan wasn't pushing him away.

Ian sauntered into the police station, a silly grin on his face and the bill of his baseball cap turned toward the back of his head. "Good afternoon, Sheriff," he drawled. "Shawn."

Shawn Chadwick, Skyler's only deputy, slid lower in his chair and muttered a curse as the door banged against the wall. "Hey."

Evan looked up from a mountain of paperwork. "Ian."

Shuffling toward the wooden chair opposite Evan's desk, Ian chuckled as he moved. "Heard that you got invited to have a glass of tea with the ex-missus."

Evan removed his wire-rimmed glasses and shot him a baleful look. "Where did you hear that rumor?"

"Do you really have to ask him that, Sheriff? The man's tongue wags more than the tail of every dog in Lincoln County," Shawn ground out.

Ian shrugged without taking offense and crossed his ankles, slouching down in the chair to make himself comfortable. "Don't matter where I heard it anyway, but the way I heard it, you stayed there for quite a spell."

"You shouldn't listen to gossip." Evan returned his attention to his work.

Ian sniffed. "Came straight from Diane Tanner's mouth."

Evan's head shot up. "What?"

"Yep. I went to the bakery to grab myself some doughnuts this morning and she was just chattering on and on about how you and Morgan spent some time together yesterday afternoon and that coming back here was the best thing for her daughter." Ian waggled bushy eyebrows. "Sounds like she's ready to start baking another wedding cake."

Evan threw his pen down and pushed himself to his feet. He rounded his desk and leveled a glare at the older man. "Morgan is back in Skyler to recover from her injuries and get her life back in order. She didn't come back here to rekindle anything. There's nothing to be rekindled. Morgan and I are friends now, just as we were in the past. Friends. Got it?"

Ian squeaked out a response. "Got it." But Evan knew the old man was trying hard not to laugh.

Damnation. "Now, don't you have somewhere to be?"

"Yep." Ian didn't move.

Evan swallowed his frustration. "Where?"

"I'm supposed to be fixing Mae's fence."

"I thought that was yesterday."

Ian grinned up at him. "It was, but when I didn't show up, she called me and I promised her I'd do it today. She fell for it. Now, she's waiting on me."

"Jesus," Deputy Chadwick muttered before launching himself to his feet. "Why don't you just go ahead and marry the woman? The two of you have been playing cat and mouse like this for the last three years."

Ian stood so fast the chair wobbled. He steadied it and glared at Chadwick. "Marry her? Why in hell would I want to attach myself to another ball and chain? Why, I'll have you know..."

As the argument intensified, Evan snatched his hat from the hook by the door and slammed out of the office.

Dexter balled up the last page of the newspaper and threw it across the room. It skittered on the linoleum and came to rest against one leg of the cracked coffee table.

No mention of Morgan Hennessy in any of the newspapers he'd read, and he'd read a damned lot of them. He'd searched every last, damned page. He scrubbed his spiked hair and dropped his hands back down to the kitchen table.

A woman simply did not disappear without a trace, especially not a woman with a high profile like Morgan. Dexter drummed his fingers on the table.

He'd find the bitch. No matter how long it took. She couldn't hide forever.

Morgan sifted through the compact discs she'd had her able assistant send to her once she'd started the path to recovery. Though she didn't know if she'd be able to return to work anytime soon, she needed to put the clients' files in order as best she could. The only trouble was her ability to concentrate.

She sat by the window overlooking the backyard, staring out at the lush green grass, the pine birdhouse, the berries hanging from the Solomon's seal and the rhododendrons. With the window open to allow in a cooling breeze, she caught the scent of the Japanese honeysuckle her parents constantly battled.

Morgan gave up all pretense of work and wandered toward the back door. The sun-warmed deck caressed her bare feet and she walked to the railing. She could almost find peace here if the nightmares didn't continue to plague her.

Each night carried the same demons. Dexter's hands. His voice. The wild look in his eyes as he lit the flame and the words, which changed her life.

Do you know what happens when fire comes in contact with alcohol?

She shivered despite the warmth of the day and began to back toward the doorway. Though she'd ventured into town on her own, she still didn't like being alone in the house. She almost laughed at the ludicrous thought. She'd spent the better portion of the past ten years dealing with belligerent criminals, living alone in a city ten times the size of Skyler, and now, here she was afraid to be alone in the house she was raised in. It shouldn't be this way.

She hurried back into the house anyway, securing the lock behind her. Just as she was about to sit, a movement caught her eye. She whirled around in time to see a flash of denim.

Battling panic, Morgan snatched the cordless phone and dialed, but not before she ducked down behind the table. Her heart pounding and tears welling in her eyes, she whispered to the emergency operator.

"Please help. My name is Morgan Hennessy and I'm in trouble."

Evan got the call ten minutes later and whipping his cruiser around, he snapped the lights on and released the siren. He took the back roads to Morgan's old house, dodging potholes and squirrels recklessly.

He left the car running as he barreled up the driveway to bang on the front door of the Tanners' house. "Morgan! Open the door!" When she didn't immediately respond, fear took root and he leaped over the porch railing to dash to the back of the house.

"Morgan! It's Evan!" He identified himself to lessen her terror and as he climbed the steps to the deck, Morgan managed to open the back door. He gave her the once over to make sure she was in one piece and then he dragged her into his arms. "What's wrong? What did you see?"

Morgan held onto his shirt, burying her face against his chest. "Jeans."

He tipped her face up and the tears shimmering in her green eyes caused his breath to snag in his throat. "Jeans? What do you mean? You saw someone wearing jeans?" Accustomed to prying information out of terrified witnesses and victims, Evan hated lumping Morgan into either category.

She nodded and drew in several deep gulps of air. "I was coming back in from the deck and I had just locked the door. Then I saw a flash of denim and somebody running."

Evan's jaw clenched and he took hold of her shoulders. "Morgan, I need you to think for me. Was it Dexter Canfield?"

Her face went ghastly pale. "I don't...I don't...God." She dropped her head back down to his chest.

Evan allowed her a few seconds to compose herself before he pushed her back again. "I need a description, honey. Can you give me more than jeans?"

She shook her head morosely. "I didn't watch him. I ducked."

"You ducked?"

"Down behind the table." Her lower lip wobbled.

He captured her face in his hands. "That's perfectly okay, Morgan. No one expects you to forget what's happened to you. Your natural instinct is to hide." He kissed her forehead. "And you followed your instincts. Now, I want you to stay here."

She clutched at his arm. "Where are you going?"

He placed his hand over hers. "I'm going to take a look around and call this into the station."

She expelled a loud breath and slipped her hand out from beneath his. "I'm sorry. I know you have a job to do."

"Morgan, I'll come back," he promised.

She stumbled toward the table and sat. "Do you really think it could be Dexter?"

He gave her what he hoped was a reassuring smile. "No, I don't. The police have taken great pains to keep your whereabouts secret. No one knows you're here except for the same people you grew up with and you can trust us. Hell, even Kenny Brower called me about posting a sentry at the edge of town to keep a lookout, and you know Kenny wouldn't get involved if he didn't care about you."

Morgan folded her hands atop the table. "I know. He's a good man."

Evan had never heard Kenny described that way, but he didn't contradict her. At least the fear had begun to recede from her eyes. "Do you want me to get you something before I take a look around?"

"He's probably gone by now," she whispered.

"They always leave clues."

Her eyes whipped up and Evan cursed himself for talking like a cop. "I mean—" he tried to correct his mistake, but Morgan shook her head.

"I know what you mean, Evan. In this case, I hope you do find some clues."

"Sit tight." He backed toward the door, keeping his gaze trained on her face. "I just want you to sit there and wait for me, okay?"

Morgan closed her laptop and scooted the discs away from the edge of the table. "I'll be right here."

The front door slammed and Diane came racing into the sunroom, panic in her eyes. Evan held up one hand in an attempt to calm her down, but Diane had already captured Morgan in a bear hug.

"Oh my God, when Ellie called from the post office and said you'd called 911, I panicked!" Diane brushed her hands over Morgan's hair and kissed her cheeks. "Are you all right?"

Evan figured now was as good a time as any to finish his job. He turned and placed one hand on the doorknob. He barely made it onto the deck when he heard the bloodcurdling scream.

He shot a look over his shoulder and then back toward the yard and, with his heart hammering in his chest, he drew his .9mm and leveled it.

"Freeze!"

Morgan bumped her shoulder against her mother's as she jumped to her feet. She ran to the back door to get a better look, but Evan's harsh, "stay back," froze her in her tracks.

Across the grass, she saw a pair of lifted hands, a ratty T-shirt and equally torn jeans, but Morgan focused on the hair. Thick, dark hair. She sagged against the wall with relief. "It's not him."

Evan spared her a glance. "You're sure?"

She heard the disappointment in his voice. Evan wanted to catch Dexter Canfield as much as she wanted him to get caught. "Dexter has a crew cut, blond hair and he's about six inches taller. I don't recognize this guy."

"Stay back." Evan issued the order again as he advanced down the deck. "Keep your hands where I can see them."

Diane came to stand beside Morgan, wrapping one arm around her waist. "Well, if he's not Dexter, then I wonder who in the hell he is and what right he has trespassing on my property."

"I'm sure Evan will find out, Mom."

"Oh, I'm sure he will, too. Then, we'll fry the bastard."

As Evan got closer, he cursed. "Brandon Kenshaw, what in the hell are you doing out here? Don't you realize you could have gotten shot?"

Brandon, a panicked look on his young face, waved his arms wildly. "Don't shoot me, Sheriff Hennessy!"

"I'm not going to shoot you. Put your damned arms down." Evan returned his gun to his holster. "But you haven't answered my question."

Brandon darted a look toward the copse of trees behind the Tanners' house. "It was a dare. Honest."

Evan felt his temper beginning to climb. "You let me decide if you're being honest. Who dared you?"

The teenager licked his lips. "The Bailey brothers."

Evan folded his arms and pinned a serious look on his face, one designed to make juvenile delinquents quiver. It never failed him in New York. "Oh, they did, did they? Well, when did they issue this dare?"

Brandon stuffed his hands into the pockets of his jeans and dropped his shoulders. "Today."

"When today?" Evan's voice hardened.

"About an hour ago." The teenager's voice squeaked.

"All right. That's it. Turn around and put your hands behind your back."

"What? What are you doing, Sheriff? I'm telling the truth!"

Evan removed the handcuffs attached to his belt. "Bullshit. The Bailey brothers left last night for Charlotte with their mother. They won't get back until Sunday. In case you're wondering how I know, Mrs. Bailey's car broke down and she had to call me for assistance since her husband was at work. Now," Evan clamped a hand on Brandon's shoulder, "do you want to try again? And this time, make it the truth."

"Can I turn around?" Brandon sounded as if he were seconds away from tears.

Evan dropped his hand. "By all means. Make yourself comfortable."

"Not damned likely," Brandon muttered.

"Well? I'm waiting."

Brandon started to inch toward the back fence.

"Don't make me chase you, Brandon. You wouldn't like it when I caught you."

The boy's breath wheezed out of his lungs. "I don't know his name. Just some guy said he was a reporter and he offered me five hundred dollars to get close enough to the Tanners' house to plant this." He dug into the pocket of his jeans and produced a small, silver button.

Evan snagged it for closer inspection. "A bug. This reporter wanted you to plant a bug in Morgan's house. And you agreed?"

Brandon shuffled his feet. "It was five hundred bucks, Sheriff!"

Evan didn't give him the chance to turn around again. He walked behind the boy and secured his hands with the silver bracelets.

"I thought you weren't going to take me in!"

"I never said that." Evan gave him a light push. "Start walking. My car's out front. Probably out of gas by now because of this stupid ass stunt."

Brandon walked, whining all the way. Once situated in the back seat of the cruiser, the teen peeked up at Evan. "Do you have to call my parents?"

"You're sixteen. You figure it out, but while you're figuring, tell me where to find this reporter friend of yours."

"I never said he was my friend."

"Brandon." Evan's patience slipped another notch.

"He said he'd meet me behind the motel at seven tonight. If I'd done the job right, he'd give me my money."

Evan leaned down until he was eye level with the teen. "You're lucky I caught you, Brandon."

"Why? Now I'm out the money and my dad's going to kick my ass."

"It's better than a bullet between the eyes." Evan slapped the window and straightened, walking around to the driver's side to call in the arrest and kill the engine.

"A reporter?" Morgan sank down onto the sofa. "I thought we'd kept this from the media."

Evan knelt in front of her and took her hands in his. "I don't even know if this guy really is a reporter. He could simply be someone out to make a quick buck with a tabloid. I'm going to meet with him at seven tonight and then I'll know more."

"Take plenty of bullets," Diane Tanner instructed in a cold tone.

Evan cleared his throat. "For now, Morgan, I think it's best if you stay inside the house."

"Where else would I go?" She fidgeted with the hem of her blouse. "I feel like a caged animal. The only difference is, I don't want out of my cage."

Evan slid his hand up alongside her jaw and for a brief moment, Morgan allowed herself to accept his comfort. "I'll check back in with you later on this evening." He withdrew his hand and stood. "Diane, make sure you keep all the doors locked and it might not be a bad idea to call Jack and ask him to come home."

"Ask hell," Diane muttered as she turned away.

Evan chuckled. "Your mother has that same spark I see in you."

"I'd be surprised if you see it now."

Evan leaned down and kissed the top of her head. "We're going to get you through this, baby. I promise."

She looked up at him and the softness in his hazel eyes warmed her, comforted her more than words. She knew she could count on Evan. No matter the cost, he would protect her. She got up to stand in front of him. "Be careful when you go tonight."

He patted his gun. "I take careful with me wherever I go." He winked.

She snatched hold of his hand and squeezed his fingers. "I mean it, Evan. Promise me."

He looked down at their joined hands for a long second before he responded. "I promise."

As Morgan watched him walk away, a deep, abiding sense of foreboding slid its way into the pit of her stomach.

Dexter propped his feet on the personnel director's desk. Seeing as how the old biddy wouldn't be working any longer, he doubted she'd mind him making himself at home, but just in case, he asked politely, "Mrs. Austin, you don't mind, do you?" He cackled at his own humor and set to work.

He flicked open the file folder and began to peruse the contents. "Now, if I was a scared attorney with a scarred body, where would I go?"

The tiny desk lamp provided little light, but all Dexter needed was a little light. He hummed his way through all of Morgan's personal assessments and evaluations and studied her salary increases with a twinge of anger. "Damned bitch made twice as much as I did."

Then he moved on to her original resume. "Oh, yes. Now, we're getting somewhere. A graduate of North County High School. Skyler, North Carolina."

He closed the file and returned it to its proper place in the metal drawer. Then, with casual movements, he switched off the lamp, stepped over Mrs. Austin's prone body and whistled his way out of the office.

Chapter Four

Evan slumped down low in his Dodge pickup and tugged the ball cap over his eyes. Night had fallen across the town and the clock crawled closer to seven. He didn't take his eyes off the back entrance to the motel and at precisely two minutes before the hour, a shadowy figure rewarded his patience.

Evan climbed out of his pickup and crept slowly across the parking lot while the man paced the length of the back wall of the motel.

"Are you waiting for someone?" Evan carried the element of surprise and the man leaped around, his hands extended in front of him as if to ward off an attack.

"Who in the hell are you?" The man spit out the words as he backtracked toward the exit passageway.

Evan opened the front of his jacket and showed the badge clipped to his belt. "Sheriff Hennessy. And you are?"

"Aw, hell."

"Funny name," Evan commented before strolling forward. He crooked his finger and pointed toward the wall. "Get back over here. You and I have something to discuss."

"Look, I don't want any trouble."

"Really? Then you picked a hell of a way to find it." Evan reached out and grasped a handful of the thick, denim shirt and dragged the man into the glow of the streetlight. He didn't recognize the craggy features. "Now, I'll ask you nicely. Who are you and what are you doing in my town?" He bumped the man's shoulders against the brick. "And before you think about lying to me, I should tell you that the boy you hired to bug Morgan Hennessy's house is now in custody singing like a tenor at choir practice. So let's start from the top." Evan bumped him again. "And let me warn you, I don't have a lot of patience tonight."

"I'm Dub Edwards and..."

"Dub?"

The man shifted uncomfortably. "Childhood nickname. It stuck. Real name is Harry."

"Okay, Harry Edwards, let's go to part two of my questions. What are you doing here?"

"Look, I need money and that Hennessy woman is worth a lot of it, especially with the right material. Why, there's newspapers offering ten thousand dollars for just one picture. I thought they'd pay a hell of a lot more than that to hear a conversation about the attack." His eyes widened when Evan's face came into his line of vision. "What are you doing?"

"Now that you've answered my questions, I have no more use for you." Evan unsnapped his holster.

"What?" Harry crammed himself against the wall. "You can't kill me! That's police brutality!"

"Do you have family, Harry?"

The man shook his head. "Never married."

"Then who's going to report your disappearance?" Evan released the safety on his weapon.

Harry tried to break away, but Evan lifted his knee and held him in place. Then, placing the barrel of his .9mm against Harry's skull, Evan asked, "Who hired you?"

Harry managed to find some bluster and responded with an epithet.

Evan braced his forearm over Harry's windpipe. "I'm sorry. I didn't hear your response. Perhaps you'd like to try again, keeping in mind that my patience has just slipped another notch. And believe me when I tell you that you don't want to be around when I run out of it."

Harry's gaze darted toward both ends of the hotel before returning to Evan's face. "Just some newspaper guy I know. He said he could make us a million if I did all the hard work. I knew I couldn't get close enough to the Tanners' house without raising a few eyebrows so I hired the kid. Dumbass actually thought he was going to get paid." He snickered.

Evan considered punching him. "Actually, I think he was the smart one in the bunch." He twisted his fist in Harry's collar and began tugging him away from the wall.

"Where are we going?"

"I'm taking you for a steak dinner. Where in the hell do you think we're going? I'm taking you to jail."

Harry slumped alongside him. "You know, I could probably talk the guy into cutting you in on the profits."

Evan didn't restrain himself this time and as Harry clutched his nose and howled with pain, Evan felt only marginally better.

Morgan wouldn't admit she waited by the phone for Evan's call, but the second it rang, she snatched up the cordless. "Hello?"

"We have the guy in custody," Evan said without preamble.

She breathed a little easier. "So what happens now?"

"We go after the guy who hired him."

She swallowed hard and rubbed her temples. "Someone else is involved?"

"Yeah. This guy isn't smart enough to be the mastermind, but he gave up his employer's name. I've called a friend of mine with the FBI, and he's going to track the joker down. We'll get him, but you're safe. This is no more than someone trying to make a few bucks off a..." His voice trailed off.

"Off what? A tragedy? That was what you were going to say, wasn't it?"

"I'm sorry."

She swiftly changed the subject. "How did he find me, Evan? How did he know this is my hometown?"

"From what I understand, it was in an old interview you did shortly after being hired by Baker and Snyder."

Morgan groaned. "So we don't even know if he's told anyone else. My parents could be in danger. I have to leave." Tucking the phone next to her ear, she launched herself to her feet. "I need to leave. I'm going to pack now."

"Morgan." Evan's voice flowed across the line, calm, reassuring. "Nothing has happened. According to the guy I caught tonight, no one has said anything because they were too busy trying to get all the money for themselves. They hoped to sell a story about you to some rag and make a ton of money."

Morgan still walked toward the stairs. "Coming here was a bad idea."

"No, it wasn't."

"You don't know that, Evan." She sounded hysterical to even her own ears.

"Listen to me..." he began.

"Don't try to pacify me!" She made it to the top of the stairs and holding the phone close to her ear, she lowered her voice to keep her parents from hearing. "You can't solve every problem, Evan."

"I'm not trying to solve every one. Just this one."

"I shouldn't have come here expecting you to protect me."

"Is that the reason you came?"

Her breath exploded out of her lungs as she realized her mistake. She gripped the cordless receiver tighter. "I have to go."

"What are you going to do?"

"I'm not sure."

Evan remained quiet for a long second before adding, "Morgan, don't leave. I can't protect you hundreds of miles away from here. Besides that, where would you go? Do you really want to go back to your home in Raleigh?"

The mere thought sent slivers of terror skating down her spine like tiny ice picks. She didn't know where she would go, but staying here no longer seemed plausible. "I can't depend on you to save me from this lunatic."

"Sure you can. It's what I do."

His words stung a little. As much as Evan claimed they were still friends, she had to wonder if he was only helping her now out of a sense of duty, but she wouldn't ask him. "I think I know that better than anyone."

"Are you going to bed now?" She didn't have long to think about what he was really asking because Evan continued talking. "Or would you like to go grab a cup of coffee? The diner stays open until two or so."

She knew she should tell him she was going to bed. She needed to avoid Evan at all costs. She hadn't returned to Skyler to resume any type of relationship with him and spending time with him would only muddy the waters. Still, she found herself responding affirmatively. "Coffee sounds good."

"I'll pick you up in ten."

They were alone in the diner except for the waitress and the cook, both of whom were seated at the counter enjoying a cup of coffee themselves.

Evan lifted a hand to wave at both of them when he walked in behind Morgan. He held up two fingers to indicate coffee and led her to a booth in the far corner of the diner.

"This place hasn't changed much," Morgan noted as she slid across the cracked upholstery. She took the side of the booth facing the door, putting the left side of her body out of the line of sight.

"It's a staple here." Evan smiled at her as he moved the laminated menu out of the way and folded his arms across the table.

The waitress approached with two steaming cups of coffee. "Hiya, Evan. Good to see you. Morgan, hadn't seen you in quite some time."

Morgan lifted her eyes and Evan quickly supplied the woman's name. "You remember Jane, don't you, Morgan?"

Morgan nodded slightly, though Evan clearly saw she had no recollection of the woman. "It's good to see you again, Jane." She lowered her eyes once more and Evan saw her tug on the edge of the turtleneck to make sure it was securely in place.

Jane set the mugs down in front of them. "What else can I get for you?"

"I think we only want coffee right now. We'll give you a holler if we change our minds." Evan waited until the waitress walked away before he directed his gaze back toward Morgan. "She was married to Buddy Walker, the high school quarterback."

Recognition dawned in her eyes. "Oh. I thought they moved to Dallas. The last I heard he'd gotten a job with a high tech firm and was making his way in the world."

Evan lowered his voice. "Yeah, he did. Unfortunately, he decided to do it without Jane."

Morgan winced. "That's why she's still working here."

He took a sip of the strong, black coffee. "Some people find comfort here." He looked at her over the rim of the cup. "Is that why you came back?"

She stirred cream into the mug and added two packs of sugar. Just as he remembered. "I think the jury's still out on that one."

He smiled. "Do you think you'll work with your mother at the bakery while you're here?"

"I'm not sure. A part of me wants to just hide out."

"And you already know that's not the best thing to do. I'm sure I don't need to tell you that victims need to face the situation."

Her hand tightened around the mug. "I'm not a victim."

Evan amended his statement. "And with people trying not to be victims."

She didn't relax her spine, and Evan wondered if coming here was such a good idea after all. "I don't want to think about it."

"But it won't let you stop thinking about it, will it?"

Her hair draped over the left side of her face as she leaned forward. "The dreams are so vivid at times. I can still see his face." She stirred her coffee with the spoon and her face took on a faraway look. He knew she'd left him then, retreating back into the protective shell she'd wrapped herself in since the attack.

He reached across the table and covered her hand with his. "Morgan."

Startled, she looked up, blinked, as if surprised to see him sitting across from her.

"You came to the right place," he told her in the softest of voices.

She withdrew her hand slowly. "That remains to be seen."

Evan leaned back against the upholstery, assuming a relaxed posture. He wanted to put her at ease. He'd never had to try before. "Tell me about working for Baker and Snyder."

She dipped her finger in the sugar that had dropped on the rim of the mug and brought the digit to her mouth. Evan's body went on full alert the second those plum-colored lips circled the tip of her finger. She lifted her shoulders in a careless shrug and her green eyes clouded. "It was a job."

"Not a career?"

"Let's just say it wasn't what I expected."

He clenched his hand around a packet of sugar to keep from reaching for her. "Is anything ever what we expected?"

She lifted her head and her lip curled upwards in a slight smile. "Philosophy from you?"

He chuckled. "You might not be the only one who's changed."

"Maybe not." She drew in a deep breath. "Evan, why did you ask me out for coffee?"

"Was I not supposed to?"

She frowned. "I didn't say that. I'm just wondering if there was an ulterior motive. We haven't talked this much since the week before I left."

Her words reminded him of the hard, cold dose of reality he'd gotten the day he'd realized she'd really left. "Just because we aren't married anymore doesn't mean I don't care about you."

"Thanks."

Evan heard the distinctive sound of a door closing, effectively shutting him out. Morgan had probably made a list of things she wouldn't talk about and their marriage topped the list, no doubt, a close second to Dexter Canfield's attack.

Evan's stomach knotted. He didn't want to know all the gory details. The news media had helpfully provided more than he would ever need, but he knew Morgan needed to release the fear or she would never be whole again. He doubted she'd appreciate hearing that kernel of wisdom from him. That knowledge didn't stop him from trying.

He cleared his throat. "Do you remember when I got shot the first time?"

Her head shot up. "I couldn't exactly forget that. When the captain called me and told me you were on the way to the hospital, I thought my heart would stop."

"How much do you remember about my recovery?"

Her brows knitted. "You were a bear. You've never made a good patient." She stopped talking and for a long second, simply stared at him. When he didn't look away, she finally asked, "Evan, where is this going?"

He kept his gaze on hers, steady, unblinking. "I believe someone very wise told me I needed to get professional help, to talk about what had happened to me, or I wouldn't escape the memories...or the fear."

A long sigh filled the air. "Touché."

"I'm not trying to score points. I'm trying to help."

She took her time sipping her coffee before responding. "I appreciate it. I really do, but if I need help, I'll ask for it."

He gave her a disbelieving look. "Since when? You've never been one to ask for help."

She held up one hand and Evan saw the shakiness. "Could we talk about something else, please?"

Frustration climbed its way up his spine, but he reluctantly gave in. He had no choice. Morgan knew how to get her way. Avoidance was usually her weapon of choice. "Okay, what would you like to talk about?"

"Tell me about you."

Evan allowed the conversation to drift. They talked about his return to Skyler, his duties as the sheriff of Skyler, and the house he'd purchased, but the topic never returned to Morgan. She wouldn't allow it, at least not anything she considered too personal. She touched on some cases she'd handled, a couple of friends she had in Raleigh and even brought up the subject of dating, though she hadn't really managed to make it past the second date.

Evan didn't stay on that subject for long. The thought of Morgan dating anyone else snagged his stomach in knots. He wanted to ask if those guys had kissed her goodnight. Then he wanted to track each one of them down and tell them to stay away from his wife. Only, she wasn't his wife anymore.

Evan kept his hand at the small of her back as he walked her up the steps to the front door of her parents' house. Morgan remembered when he used to do that when they were dating. They'd sit on the porch swing for hours and though Evan had often been the recipient of razzing for his choice of activities, he'd never allowed it to bother him.

Morgan smiled as they reached the top step. "Do you remember the first time my father caught us out here kissing?"

Evan's laughter created a warmth in the pit of her stomach. "How could I forget? He practically chased me off the steps and threatened to skin me if he ever caught me out here again."

"Well, I was only fifteen." She thought she'd give anything to go back to those days, to the carefree innocence of youth and the mild rebellion of her teen years. At the time, she thought the angst and misery were the worst things she could ever endure. She couldn't have been more wrong. She looked over at Evan and shook her head. "God. Fifteen. I can't even believe it myself."

Evan braced his back against a white pillar and continued to smile. "You were a very mature fifteen."

She rolled her eyes. "I don't remember you using that line on Dad."

"I didn't think he'd appreciate it."

Morgan laughed, startling them both. She couldn't remember the last time she'd laughed. Even before Dexter's attack, laughter hadn't been a part of her daily life. She spent most of her time working and there simply wasn't time for hilarity.

"What are you thinking?" Evan's voice broke into her thoughts.

She lifted her shoulders in a shrug, wanting to change the subject before her morose thoughts ended the evening on a note she didn't want. She walked toward Evan and touched his arm lightly. "Thank you."

He raised one eyebrow and the glow of the front porch light captured the curiosity in the hazel eyes she'd always loved. "For what?"

"For not expecting more than I can give right now."

His gaze dropped to her lips and Morgan's nerves began to jangle. She wondered if he was going to kiss her and then prayed he would. She'd never forgotten the first taste of his lips...or the last. Both had been equally devastating. Unconsciously, she leaned in closer.

Evan took hold of her shoulders and Morgan's eyelids began to drift. Then she felt the brush of his lips on her forehead. Her eyes flew open and she thought she saw a brief glimpse of mischief in his eyes. Disappointment spiraled through her, but she quickly shuttered her emotions by delivering a kiss to Evan's cheek followed by a firm hug.

"I guess I'll see you tomorrow."

He cupped her cheek and his thumb grazed the groove of her mouth. "I won't tell you things will look better in the morning."

"Things will be better when this is all over."

He curled a lock of her hair around two fingers just as he used to do when they'd dated. He'd always loved her hair. He'd told her many times. Now, the memory came back to haunt her.

"Sweet dreams, Mrs. Hennessy," he whispered.

The words caught her off-guard but before she had time to dwell on them, Evan twisted the doorknob and swept open the door.

"Oh, and Morgan?"

She paused with one foot inside the door. "Yes?" She spoke so quietly she wondered if he heard her.

"I did want to kiss you goodnight just then."

Her heart began to pound. "I guess you had your reasons why you didn't."

"It's not the one you're thinking."

She looked back then, one eyebrow raised. She needed his explanation, one that wouldn't send her to her room to dwell in the remnants of misery awaiting her there. "So what is it then?"

His hand reached for her hair again and she wondered if he could see the frantic rise and fall of her breasts. "Because one kiss wouldn't be enough." He allowed the strand to drop and he took a step away from her. "You'd better get inside before we wake your parents again...just like old times."

Morgan somehow forced her legs to carry her further into the foyer. She said goodnight over her shoulder while Evan stood on the porch.

She turned to close the door and he still stood there. "What are you doing?"

"I'll leave when you close the door."

Morgan didn't stop smiling until she reached her bedroom.

Chapter Five

Morgan wanted to avoid the doorbell when it rang early the next morning. But as the summons continued, she tiptoed to the top of the stairs. "Mom?" She checked her watch. Just after ten in the morning. Her mother would have been at the bakery for at least three hours. The doorbell rang again, telling her the morning visitor wasn't going away anytime soon.

Tucking the towel closer around the top of her breasts she came down a few more stairs, trying to catch a glimpse through the beveled glass next to the door. When the pealing continued, she finally gave up and stormed down the stairs.

She swept the door wide and her freshly prepared greeting dropped to the ground like hailstones. "Evan? What are you doing here?" She clutched the towel even tighter and tried to fade into the shadows afforded by the heavy drapes covering the bay windows.

"I believe you have a doctor's appointment this morning." Evan stepped into the slim space she'd allotted him and leaned in close to her bare neck. "You smell great."

Realization hit. Her neck and upper body were well exposed to Evan's view as were the thick scars. With a curse, she turned around and sped up the stairs. Racing down the hallway, she cursed herself as much as Evan. She should have grabbed a robe. She should have covered herself better.

"Hey! Where are you going?" He clumped up the stairs behind her. She heard his boots thumping on the carpet and she slammed the bedroom door.

"I'm getting dressed. You still haven't told me what you're doing here and you should have called first."

"I thought you might need a ride and what's this about calling first? I've never done that before."

He was right. "Things change, Evan."

"Duly noted. Still thought you might like a lift."

"Try again. I've been driving for twenty years."

He tapped lightly on the bedroom door. "Are you going to let me in?"

"I'm getting dressed."

"That's precisely why I asked."

Morgan paused, her hands fisting around the edge of the comforter covering the same bed she'd slept in when she was a teenager. "Evan, what do you want?"

"I thought I'd told you that already."

"And why don't I believe it was the truth?" She heard something bump against the wooden door and wondered if it was his head. He always used to do that when they were fighting. He'd stand outside her bedroom door, his forehead pressed to the wood and implore her to come out and talk to him. She needed to stop dwelling on the memories. They served no purpose now.

"You sound angry."

"I wasn't expecting company." She threw the damp towel toward her bed and yanked the first thing she came to her in her closet, another turtleneck, this one ribbed and scarlet red. It suited her mood. She shoved her legs into her jeans. "Like I said, you should have called first."

"Is that really what's got you so riled up? You're mad because I didn't call first?" He sounded incredulous. "Come on. That never used to bother you."

She dragged the hairbrush through her tangled hair. "Yes, it did. I never told you. It's called common courtesy." She didn't regret the lie. She needed the distance it gave her...or at least, hoped it would give her. Evan was moving in too close. She couldn't allow that.

"I see." His voice told her he didn't really. "Is this because I dropped by or because you didn't have your usual barriers in place?"

Infuriated, she snatched open the door. "Barriers?"

He leaned against the doorframe, his manner relaxed, casual. He didn't look concerned in the least and that made her even angrier. "Yeah. You know. Like this." He tugged at the collar of her shirt.

She smacked his hand away. "They're called clothes."

"You dress like you're in the Antarctica."

She slammed the door again.

"And you're acting like a child," he added.

"You didn't just come to give me a ride. So you want to tell me what's really going on?" She heard his foot thump against the lower half of the door.

"Your mom called me." The door opened again and Evan whirled in time to keep from staggering back into her bedroom. "Thanks for the warning."

"You mean, like you gave me this morning?"

"This isn't about my visit, is it? It's about my seeing the scars."

As Evan said the words, the blood rushed to Morgan's face. "Don't." She gave the verbal smack as a first line of attack, an attempt to ward off any thoughts of touching her...or the scars.

He raised one eyebrow. "Don't what?"

"Talk to me about the scars. I don't want to discuss them with you."

Evan snorted and took a step toward her. "You don't want to discuss them with anyone, even your doctors. Look, I know it was a difficult time for you and—"

She gave an abrupt, bitter laugh. "Difficult? Is that how you describe it? Difficult was the ending of our marriage, Evan. This," she lifted up the hem of her shirt to show him the angry scars traversing the length of her left side, "was excruciating. I've never endured agony like this before and I hope to hell I never have to go through this again." She squared her shoulders and prepared to close the door, but Evan wedged his foot into the space. She glared at him. "Go back to work. I can drive myself to your father's office. My mother had no business calling you."

"You're not the only one hurting, Morgan. When your mother lays awake at night listening to your sobs, do you think she doesn't hurt, too?"

Morgan managed to keep from visibly wincing. She'd hoped her mother hadn't heard the tears. "I'll talk with my mother, but I'm done with you."

He pushed one hand against the door and Morgan stepped back out of the way. She couldn't stop him from coming into the room, but she didn't have to stay and listen to his lecture. She turned around and walked toward the adjoining bathroom, but Evan caught up with her before she could escape.

"Let go of me," she instructed when his hand tightened around her wrist.

"You came back to Skyler because I asked you to," Evan began.

"So what if I did?"

"As much as you hate to admit it, you want me to help you."

"Maybe I had a moment of weakness." His aftershave tickled her nostrils and behind her, she felt the solid wall of his chest. His arms went around her waist and pulled her back against him. She wanted to lean into him, to allow him to absorb some of her fears, to make things better. He'd always been able to soothe her in the past, but that was then. Now, things were different. She was different. Even he couldn't fix that.

"I have a confession to make," he whispered in her ear.

"What?" The warmth of his palm pressed against her abdomen loosed an entire army of butterflies in her stomach.

"I'm having a moment of weakness right now." His fingers crawled under the edge of her shirt and Morgan sucked in a sharp breath. "Easy," he soothed, drawing his fingertips over the ridges in her skin. He nibbled her ear gently and liquid heat pooled between her legs. Evan could always make her feel like a sensual woman. Her head fell back against his chest.

"You shouldn't be...we shouldn't be..." she whispered, not quite sure what she intended to say. She only knew what she wanted—to let go, to give herself the luxury of feeling like a woman again, instead of a frightened shell.

Evan turned her in his arms, cupping her face with his palms. "When have we ever followed rules?" His thumbs stroked the corners of her mouth.

She closed her eyes, anticipating the kiss. Pure silk. Sweet. Hot. Powerful. His lips swept over hers with mastery, domination and yet, surrender. She tasted his mouthwash and

65

felt his tongue glide over hers in an intimate slow dance. He held her gently, like a fragile piece of glass, while she wanted to push him back against the wall and demand he take her. She needed to feel like a woman again. She needed...Evan. She stood on tiptoe to accommodate the difference in their heights and clutched her hands into the cotton material of his shirt.

He broke the kiss with a curse, holding her at arm's length. The abrupt shift in mood confused her and she blinked up at him, into the depths of his slumberous hazel eyes. "What's wrong?" The words sounded choppy, broken.

Evan touched his forehead to hers. "You have a doctor's appointment."

She still couldn't think and his scent enveloped her, making her knees weak. "Is that really why you stopped?"

He kissed the soft skin just below her hairline. "I didn't want to stop, Morgan, but I won't take advantage of you like this."

She pushed him away, her ire spiking. "Did you ever stop to think that maybe I'm the one taking advantage or that maybe, just maybe, I wanted this? You know what? Never mind. Go back to work. I can drive myself to your father's office." She took a few steps away from him.

"Wait a second." He tried to snatch her arm, but she was too quick for him this time. She made it into the bathroom and with a final, "go away, Evan," slammed the door.

He smacked his palm against the heavy wood. "No. I'm not going away. You can tell me to get lost all you want, Morgan, but I'm not leaving you. This is my town and you came back here, remember? You need me."

She turned the water on to drown out the sound of his voice. As much as she hated to admit it, he was right. She did need him, and more than just his ability to protect her. Once upon a time, she trusted Evan, knew she could turn to him and he would take care of everything. She'd never lost that feeling.

She just hoped it wouldn't be her downfall now.

Dexter took a hearty swig of the cheap liquor. Hair of the dog. He shuddered as the metallic whiskey burned its way down his throat. His head pounding, he crawled his way out of the rickety bed and staggered to the lone window in the bedroom. One peek out at the street told him he wouldn't be leaving anytime soon.

Police combed the streets of Raleigh, searching for him under every rock, and travel wasn't safe, not even in the middle of the night. Dexter cursed his luck and slapped the curtain back into place. Since he'd killed that old secretary, the cops had been scurrying around like roaches.

He caught a glimpse of his reflection in the mirror and grinned. "You look like hell, old boy." Red-streaked eyes set against a backdrop of pale skin covered with two days' growth of beard. He hadn't washed his hair in a couple of days. He sniffed his armpits. "Whooooo. I guess I'd better make time for that shower today. I want to be smelling fresh and clean when I finally make it to Skyler."

He strolled past the mirror and dug into the brown paper bag at the foot of the bed for a clean pair of shorts. He tucked the plain blue boxers under his arm and strolled toward the bathroom.

As he stepped beneath the warm spray of the water, he closed his eyes and sighed with pleasure. "I think I might just have to wait to kill you, Morgan, my sweet." He turned to face the heated jets. "My imagination is running wild with me." He cackled aloud. "I think that would be a very good idea, indeed.

My sweet, beautiful Morgan. I can't wait to have you in my arms."

Morgan sat in the waiting room of Dr. Hennessy's office, flipping through outdated magazines and shifting uncomfortably on the leather sofa. From the corner of her eye, she watched Evan watching her. When she'd walked out of the bathroom fifteen minutes after their argument, he'd been waiting for her. She hadn't expected any less.

He'd insisted on driving her in spite of her protests and finally, she gave in. Now, he hadn't taken his eyes off of her since they'd walked in, though he had decently sat a few chairs away from her. Every so often, she looked up to catch his gaze and what she saw in those devastating eyes created a maelstrom of emotions she didn't want to begin to decipher.

She finally gave up all pretense of reading and tossed the magazine aside. Folding her hands in her lap, she stared straight ahead, willing the nurse to open the door and call her back to the examining room.

Evan rose and walked toward her. She leveled a warning glance in his direction, but he kept coming. She turned her knees away from him.

He sat beside her. "You never were good at the cold shoulder, Morgan." He kept his voice low.

"I've improved." If the chair hadn't been bolted to the floor, she would have scooted it away from him just to get her point across, but she doubted that would do any good. Evan made his own rules, danced to the beat of his own drummer, and damned the consequences.

He chuckled and draped one hand over the back of the couch. "I guess you'll get around to telling me exactly how I pissed you off."

She shot him a withering look. "Now is not the time to have this discussion."

His fingers began to toy with her hair. "My intention wasn't to hurt you."

His words brought her shifting back to face him. She tugged her hair free. "Could we just talk about something else? Or better yet, let's not talk at all."

His fingers moved to the nape of her neck and began a slow, delicious assault. She shivered and bit her lower lip.

"We could talk about something else," he offered in a complacent tone.

"Evan." She didn't know if she was pleading with him or warning him.

"You must have thought about me while you were in Raleigh." His words startled her and she swung her head around to stare at him. He gave her an inquiring look.

"What makes you ask that?"

"Just a hunch."

"Just because we're divorced doesn't mean I never think about you, Evan." She tossed another desperate glance at the closed door separating the lobby from the examination rooms. Where in the hell was that nurse?

He moved his hand from her neck and she relaxed, until that same hand began stroking her knee ever so slightly. She tried to swat it away, but Evan always had a tenacious streak.

"Will you stop?"

His hand paused, but he didn't remove it. "Do you think if we'd stayed here, we could have made our marriage work?"

Morgan noticed one lady had taken particular interest in their conversation. "I think this isn't something we should be discussing right now."

Evan let out a gusty sigh. "Is there ever going to be a good time to discuss it?"

"Why do we need to talk about it? Our marriage is over, Evan."

"That's something I don't need to be reminded about."

Morgan softened marginally. "Look." She lowered her voice. "Is this something you want the entire town to hear?" She placed her hand atop his to still further movement altogether. She couldn't think when he touched her. She imagined that was his plan.

Evan appeared to be considering the question and then he finally lifted one shoulder in a half-hearted shrug. "I've never cared about what people think. You didn't use to."

The inner door swung open and Morgan heard her name. She leaped immediately to her feet and snatched her purse. "There's no need for you to wait. I'll just call Mom when I'm done. It's a nice day, too. I might like the walk. So don't feel the need to wait at all. I'll be fine." She darted toward the door, pausing to look over her shoulder and waggle her fingers as if, by doing so, she could encourage Evan to take her words at face value.

He only grinned in response and Morgan followed the nurse, knowing he'd be there waiting for her when she returned.

Evan did intend to wait until Morgan returned, but the call from the station made him change his mind. Leaving a note with the receptionist, he shot out into the bright sunshine and drove like a madman back to the police station.

Deputy Chadwick met him at the door with a faxed letter. His face wore the solemn expression of a judge preparing to deliver sentence to a convicted criminal. "It's from Raleigh's chief of police."

Evan's heart slammed against his chest and he snatched the paper from his deputy's hand to quickly scan the contents. "Christ."

"He has to know where Morgan is staying now, Evan."

Evan held up one hand to silence what he already knew. "The city is on alert right now so I doubt even Canfield can make it out without being noticed. It has to have been that damned reporter who alerted the media. Jesus. I need to talk to Morgan, make sure she stays inside."

Chadwick scratched his head and shuffled his feet, looking as uncomfortable as a small boy owning up to a transgression. "I thought you said she wasn't so easily convinced to do things she doesn't want to do."

Evan fixed him with a look. "And your point is?"

The deputy shrugged. "Seems to me she might not want you to continually solve her battles for her."

Evan's brows lowered. As much as he wanted her close by him, he really didn't know the best course of action for her. He checked his watch. "Look. This goes nowhere, understand? I don't want to put the entire town in panic mode."

Chadwick moved to the coffee pot and poured a Styrofoam cup full. He offered it to his boss, but Evan shook his head. "What are the odds Canfield doesn't have Skyler in his sights?"

"Slim and none." Evan clapped one hand on the younger man's shoulder and then walked back out the door. "Keep trying to find that reporter."

"I'll do it, but I'm telling you, that guy has done hauled ass as far as he can get from you and this town. That was probably who Harry called."

"I still want him found."

Chadwick slammed the desk drawer so hard Evan spun around. "You got something you want to say, Chadwick?"

The young deputy scrubbed the back of his neck and gave Evan a pained look. "Just that I don't see the need to waste time hunting for needles in haystacks when this town is in danger. Looks like my time would be better spent preparing Skyler for this bastard's approach."

Evan had always taken his employees' thoughts and opinions under consideration. This time would be no different. He let out an audible breath. "You don't think the reporter might have some information we need then?"

Chadwick fiddled with his holster. "I'm not saying that, Sheriff."

Evan nodded slowly. "I see. There's nothing wrong with being scared."

The deputy's head shot up and fire glazed in his eyes. "I never said I was scared. I'm here to do a job and I'll do it, but I just don't think finding that reporter is going to do us much good considering Canfield is probably already on his way here." Blue eyes blazing, the shorter man clamped his hands on his hips and thrust his chin forward, defiance in every angle of his body.

"Unless that reporter decides to come on ahead of Canfield and broadcast the entire showdown on national television." Evan waited a moment to allow his words to sink in before continuing. "It's not so much the information this guy has as what he's going to do with it. I don't want him hiding out in the bushes watching our every move so Canfield can sit on his ass in some hotel room plotting our respective demises."

Red crept up the collar of Chadwick's neck and he dropped his head as his shoulders sank. "I'm sorry, Evan. Didn't mean to question how you do the job."

Evan put his hand on the handle of the glass door. "And I didn't take it that way. I won't fault a man for speaking his mind. So now you know why I'd just as soon that reporter kept his ass out of Skyler." He pushed his way out into the sunshine.

"As much as I hate to say it, Morgan," he muttered below his breath, "you might have been better off staying away from Skyler."

He didn't doubt his abilities to protect her, but protecting her and remaining neutral were two entirely different things. He'd never told a victim to haul ass before, but this might call for a different strategy. From what he'd read about Dexter Canfield, the man made Hannibal Lecter look like one of the good guys.

He stomped on the gas and guided his pickup out into the meager traffic. As much as he wanted to protect Morgan, he knew his own limitations. Men like Canfield were wily and would strike when least expected. Dammit.

He came to a stop in the parking lot of his father's medical office just as Morgan exited the building. As he watched her walk toward him, his mind carried him back in spite of his determination to remain in the present.

Like all brides, she'd worn white the day they'd married, although they'd both already sampled the pleasures the nights could bring. His body betrayed him at the thought and when the sun splashed over the long tresses of Morgan's strawberry blonde hair, he shifted in the seat. Though she'd never believe him, to him she would always be the same beautiful woman he'd married. The same woman he loved.

Too late, he realized she was closer to the car than what he expected and she opened the car door before he could get out. Evan shifted again to ease the ache between this thighs and hoped Morgan didn't notice his uncomfortable posture.

"That didn't take too long. Are you sure my dad even examined you?" Evan needed a controlled subject until he could get his body under control.

"Briefly. He's sending me for blood work."

"Blood work?" Evan's internal alarm went off. His father didn't schedule unnecessary tests. "What does he think is wrong with you?"

She secured the seatbelt and flicked her hair over her shoulders. "It's routine, Evan. Now would you please take me home?"

He eyed her for a long moment before he put the car into reverse. "I'll take you home, but then we need to talk." The ache hadn't receded.

Her head fell back against the rest. "I'm all talked out."

He reached over and took her hand. "I'm sorry, but it's necessary."

Morgan rolled her head toward him. "It's about Dexter, isn't it?" She closed her eyes. "He's found me."

As much as he wanted to protect her, Evan wouldn't lie to her. "Not yet, he hasn't."

She tugged her hand free. "I shouldn't have come back."

He didn't argue with her no matter how much he wanted to. "We can talk about it after we've gotten lunch and we both have clearer heads."

"I'm not very hungry."

That didn't surprise him. Morgan always shied away from food when she was anxious. "We'll get something light."

"Still as stubborn as ever." Her comment brought a smile to his lips.

"You always liked that about me," he reminded her. "You said it gave you someone to practice your persuasive techniques on."

The only sound in the car came from the hum of the air conditioner. Morgan remained silent long enough to make him wonder if she'd fallen asleep.

"Morgan?"

"Hmmm?"

"You okay?"

She turned her head to look out the window. "Never better."

The words, dipped in bitterness, made Evan flinch. He wanted to comfort her, hold her, protect her, but most of all, he just wanted her. He wasn't surprised the feelings had remained so strong over the years. He'd never met another woman who challenged him like Morgan and definitely never one who loved as she did.

He brought her hand to his mouth and kissed her palm. "We'll figure something out."

"You should be thinking of how to protect this entire town, not just one woman."

"I don't think of you as just one woman."

"What do you think of me as then?"

"My wife."

Chapter Six

Morgan didn't know how to respond or even if Evan wanted her to respond. She sat very still for a long time before finally taking a deep breath. She opened her mouth to speak, thought better of it, and promptly closed it.

Evan finally broke the tension. "Relax, Morgan. I didn't say it to scare you."

"You did anyway." How could she explain the depth of emotion his words evoked? She desperately wanted to tell him she'd never forgotten that role. She'd loved being his wife...at least for a while. Then they'd stopped communicating and the marriage, along with her belief in happily ever after, had failed.

"You were my wife."

She didn't imagine the shortness of his tone. She figured her next words would only increase his ire. "Were being the operative word."

His jaw tightened. "I didn't need that reminder."

"We've been down this road one too many times, Evan. Our marriage didn't work out. You were the one who said we could be friends." *Please stop.* She didn't want to beg him aloud, but she needed him to stop. She couldn't discuss their failed marriage on top of all her other problems.

He clenched his hands around the steering wheel until Morgan saw white knuckles. "You've made your point."

"I've pissed you off."

"It's not like you've never done it before."

Morgan had to smile at that. She and Evan had some major arguments during their three-year marriage and they always enjoyed the hell out of making up. Except for the last one. They never made up from the last fight they had. That was the night she left.

For the longest time, she'd wondered why he hadn't come after her. It wasn't fair for her to want him to, but the old Evan, the one she'd known since grade school, would have moved heaven and hell to get to her. It had taken her a couple of years to understand Evan's reasons for letting her go.

"I never intended to stir up old memories by coming back." She wanted to touch him, but the set of his jaw warned her it wouldn't be a good idea. She clenched her hands in her lap to prevent her instincts from overruling her common sense.

"You can't stir up what's never been gone, Morgan." He slid her a glance. "And don't tell me you haven't thought about us since you've been gone."

She ducked her head. She wouldn't lie to him. Evan had been the reason why she'd thrown herself into her career instead of seeking out another relationship. She knew she'd never be able to replace him. She twisted her hands in her lap and finally responded. "I've thought about us."

"And?"

"I've wondered why we didn't work."

"We both had to want it to work."

She sensed the beginning of an argument. "And you don't think I did?"

"I didn't say that."

"You implied it."

"Hell," Evan bit out. "Look, let's just forget about this. It's not doing us any good. We've got enough problems to think about without letting our past get in our way."

Morgan moved her purse to her knees. "Why didn't you marry again?"

He swerved the car and cursed again. "Why do you ask questions like that?"

"It's a valid question, Evan. You're an attractive man. I was surprised to come back and find out you weren't married."

"Bullshit," he returned.

"What?"

"You knew I wasn't married."

She fidgeted with the strap of her designer purse. It matched her designer shoes and the sunglasses she never wore. "What makes you say that?" Playing for time was an old courtroom trick.

Evan didn't buy it. "You know as much about me as I know about you. I'll bet you even knew the day I left the force in New York."

Guilty as charged. She couldn't deny the truth so she didn't even try. She looked out the window. She noticed the elegant houses, the neatly manicured lawns and while her parents lived in a nice suburb, it wasn't this one. "Where are we going?" She sat up straighter in the seat and leaned forward to peer out the windshield. "We're nowhere near my parents' house."

"I'm taking you to my house."

She shot him a long, steady look. "And I suppose you're going to tell me why."

"I already told you. We need to talk."

"We can talk somewhere else. Let's go back to the diner." She couldn't begin to explain the butterflies dancing in her stomach. "I don't want to go to your house, Evan." Did he hear the anxiety in her voice? She'd be surprised if he didn't.

She watched his hands tighten on the steering wheel. "Tough. We need to talk without interruption and without the entire town hearing what I have to say. We can't do that at the diner at this time of the day."

Morgan fought back the panic. She was a respected member of the legal community, a strong litigator and a formidable opponent, but the thought of being alone with Evan at his home scared the wits out of her. "I repeat. I don't want to go to your house. Take me home."

"No."

She played her trump card. "I really don't feel well. I just need to lie down for a while."

"I have a guestroom." Evan wouldn't budge an inch.

She folded her arms across her chest and gave him a mutinous look he couldn't see. "This is kidnapping."

"I prefer to call it a persuasive tactic."

The teasing inflection in his voice tugged a reluctant smile from her lips. "You're an ass, Evan Hennessy."

"I work at it, Mrs. Hennessy."

Her stomach muscles knotted. He called her Mrs. Hennessy just as he used to do when they'd been married. The familiarity of the name made her heart accelerate. She used to love hearing the sound of his voice when he whispered in her ear, pushing her hair back away from her face.

Evan slowed the pickup truck to a stop in the circular driveway of a massive two-story brick home. He killed the engine and got out of the driver's side, making it around to the passenger door before Morgan could assimilate this was his house.

"Who did you kill to get this house?" she muttered as she climbed out of the truck with his assistance.

He grinned. "I invested wisely."

"If I'd known that, I would have gone after alimony."

He laughed and guided her up the front walk. "You make three times my salary."

"Not if you can afford this."

Evan stuck his key in the lock and swept open the door. "Make yourself at home. I'll make us a couple of drinks. Do you still like pink ladies?"

"I haven't changed my tastes." And she could use the restorative qualities in the gin right now. "So what do we need to talk about that we couldn't discuss at my parents' house?" She watched him walk to the gleaming chrome bar lining one side of a brick wall. She'd always liked the way he moved, with an easy, loose-limbed grace, like he was never in a hurry to get anywhere.

Evan ducked down behind the bar and straightened with a bottle of grenadine. "Two things. First, I'm taking you with me to the End of Summer Social tonight because it is my professional opinion that you need some social activity and second—" He added the cream into the mixer and held his finger over the button. "—I want you to come stay with me until Canfield is caught." The mixer came to life, giving Morgan time to assess Evan's words.

She tried to swallow past the lump in her throat. Her mouth went dry. She began to pace across the thick carpeting, her hands in the pockets of her linen slacks. "Do the police know where he is?" She asked the question just as the mixer fell silent.

"They have some leads."

"Which translated means they're just hunting like hell."

Evan poured the drinks and came toward her, handing her a frosted glass with a silver umbrella. "Here. Drink this. Sit down and relax."

She sipped the alcohol from the straw. "Relax. Now, there's something I haven't quite figured out how to do...at least not since this nightmare began."

He cupped her elbow and guided her toward the sofa. "I'd wager you haven't figured out how to do it in the past seven years. You never could do it while we were married."

Morgan sat on the edge of the leather sofa and stared up at the mantle lined with framed pictures of friends and family members. She recognized Evan's brother and parents along with a few former colleagues from the police department in New York. "Do you see any of the guys often?"

Evan took a position beside her and touched her knee. "Not really." He let out a long breath. "Morgan, we don't need to talk about Canfield if you don't want to, but we do need to talk about how to handle it if he does find you."

She held up one hand, hoping he wouldn't notice how it shook. "We can do that later. Right now, I'd rather drink my pink lady and pretend all is right with the world." She leaned back against the slick cushion and closed her eyes.

After several quiet moments, Evan asked, "How's it going?"

She cracked open one eye. "Not worth a damn. Got any ideas?"

He gave her a broad grin. "We could always have sex."

She tried to appear thoughtful then, with a careless shrug, replied, "That's only relaxing for you. I always did all the work."

Evan burst out laughing. "You could teach me then."

Morgan took another sip of the pink liquid, grateful for Evan's attempts to keep her occupied. "Old dog. New tricks."

Evan slid his hand up her thigh and goose bumps popped out over her flesh. "Wanna bet?"

She peeked up at him from beneath veiled lashes and considered his proposition. She could sink into oblivion with him, allow the pleasures of the flesh to wipe away the horrors she'd experienced, but then morning would come. And the terrors would return. She opened her mouth to speak, but Evan had already leaped to his feet. He stood in front of her, hand extended. She blinked up at him. "What are you doing?"

"Showing you where the guestroom is. You need to take a nap so you'll be ready for the shindig tonight." He gave her a wink and tugged her to her feet.

She didn't know whether she was disappointed or relieved and on the way up the stairs, as she felt Evan's hip bumping hers, disappointment won out.

He'd escaped! Dexter couldn't believe his good fortune, but all it took was one slack cop too busy to do his job. Dexter managed to slip out of the apartment with his duffel bag and a wad of cash he'd lifted from the old lady in Apartment 4D when she fell asleep in front of the television. He'd considered killing her, too, just for the sheer hell of it, but didn't want to draw any more attention to himself.

He'd slipped in and out before the old crone even broke a snore. Getting past the cops patrolling the streets hadn't been so easy, but he caught a break when a couple of hoodlums decided to rob a nearby convenience store. The next thing Dexter knew, all the heat converged on the store and not even one uniformed officer remained to notice his quiet descent from the rickety stairs onto the street.

Now, he sat behind the wheel of an extremely expensive Lincoln Navigator, another piece of stolen property, one he'd kept hidden for days until the heat died down. The cops had been too busy looking for him to care about a missing sports utility vehicle.

He pressed a button and the driver's window glided down. He held his lighter to the end of his cigarette and inhaled the acrid smoke gratefully. Nothing he liked better than a good smoke...unless it was a good kill. He imagined he'd regret not finishing off the grumpy old woman who'd lived in the dump next door to his, but he needed to learn to pace himself. He needed to keep a low profile until he found Morgan. And wouldn't she be surprised to see him?

Chuckling to himself, he passed the green road sign he'd been looking for.

Skyler, North Carolina. Four hundred miles.

The night sky twinkled with billions of stars and as Morgan walked beside Evan deep into the center of town, she wondered how she'd managed to get talked into this. After her brief nap, he'd reminded her she'd be coming home with him, but she'd quickly changed the subject and refused to even consider the idea. Thankfully, Evan had conceded, at least for now. She didn't doubt for one moment he would bring it up again.

Crickets sang lustily as they walked past a grove of bushes and Evan put his hand at the small of her back when a bustling group rushed past them.

"I'm fine." She felt the need to reassure him.

"I'm just making sure that you are. Look." He pointed toward a circle of festivities where the blaring music reached them. "They're about to start the ceremony." The scent of roasted marshmallows wafted past their noses and the sounds of jubilant laughter brought a chuckle to Morgan's lips.

She tipped her head back to see Evan's face. "Are you thinking what I'm thinking?"

He grinned wickedly. "If you're thinking about the many times we snuck away while this ceremony was going on, then, yeah."

She squeezed his fingers. "Life was so simple back then."

"Growing up always complicates things."

Morgan sucked in a sharp breath and instinctively took a step closer to Evan.

He wrapped an arm around her waist. "What's wrong?"

She kept her eyes glued straight ahead until he followed her gaze. She shifted her stance to take a backward step, but Evan prevented her from going too far. The hungry orange and blue flames mesmerized her and Morgan couldn't take her eyes off the dancing light.

"They're just lighting the torches for the ceremony. They do this every evening throughout the summer. Remember?" He slid his knuckles along her cheek. "They're not going to hurt you."

"I know," she whispered, but as one of the bearers approached, carrying the torch aloft, she struggled to breathe. The flames licked so high in the air, orange and red, wickedly hot. She knew all too well how hot they were. Her skin prickled at the memory.

"It's just Jason, Morgan. Don't you remember him? He used to always stare at you when we walked down the street." Evan must have felt Morgan's internal retreat. He held tighter to her arm. "It's okay," he soothed.

"Mrs. Hennessy, Dad told us that you were back. It's good to see you again." Jason Masters, oblivious to the fear rooting

Morgan's shoes to the concrete, took her silence as a bid for further conversation. "I know I was just fourteen when you and Sheriff Hennessy left, but I could never forget a pretty face. I always thought I'd marry you one day. Dad told me I was just being silly, but a boy can dream, can't he?" He switched the torch to his right hand, bringing the flame dangerously close to Morgan's face.

She held up one hand to ward off the heat. "Please. Don't."

"Huh?" Jason stared at her, his nose wrinkling in confusion.

Evan quickly interceded, positioning his body in between Jason and Morgan. "Jason, would you please excuse us? Right before you came up, Mrs. Hennessy was saying how thirsty she was. I'm going to take her to get a drink." He cupped Morgan's elbow while Jason bobbed his head in understanding.

"Sure, Sheriff. The drinks are straight ahead." The torch wobbled in his hand again and Morgan bit her lower lip.

Evan hurried her away. Only when the flames were a good three feet behind her did Morgan begin to relax—and she knew they were at least three feet away because she looked. She had to. Her breaths still came in short, staccato pants and her palms were damp with perspiration, but at least her muscles were starting to uncoil.

Evan guided her toward one of the benches set up for the ceremony and lowered her to the wooden seat. He knelt down in front of her. "Are you okay?"

She nodded. "I-I'm fine." But Evan knew it for the lie it was. Even she heard the shakiness of her voice and she imagined her skin had lost all of its color once the flame entered her comfort zone. Realistically, she was far from fine.

"No, you're not, but you will be." Evan climbed to his feet and sat beside her. "Maybe you should…" He stopped and cleared his throat. "There's a new psychiatrist here in town."

Morgan's teeth began to chatter. "I don't need a psychiatrist, Evan."

"It might help."

"I've already talked about all of it. In fact, I did nothing but talk about it in the hospital for seven weeks. It didn't help."

"Maybe you need longer than seven weeks."

She arched an eyebrow at him. "And maybe I just need not to think about it. We've already had this conversation. It solved nothing then, and it's not going to solve anything now."

He reached across and took hold of her hand. "Yeah, avoid it. That's always the best choice of action."

"Sarcasm. Excellent call, Evan."

He squeezed her fingers. "It was the first thing I could think of."

"Hey, Sheriff," a voice from the crowd called, "Deputy Chadwick's been looking all over for you." The man behind the voice jogged up the to the park bench. Wearing a backwards baseball cap and baggy jeans, Don Mason bent low at the waist and huffed out a breath of air. "Hiya, Morgan." He aimed his gaze on Evan. "Somethin' about a call for you." He pointed toward city hall. "I think he's holdin' it. I'll sit with Morgan for a while. Give us a chance to catch up."

Evan hesitated until Morgan waved him away. "Go take your call. Some things never change." She saw his frown but pasted a smile on her face to take the sting out of her words. "Go. I mean it."

Evan started toward city hall at a backwards run. "I'll be back in a sec. Don, keep your hands to yourself."

Don held up both hands in a gesture of surrender. "I don't know why he's never trusted me."

She managed a grin. "Possibly because you made a pass at me on our wedding day."

He plunked down on the wooden seat next to her. "I'd had a little too much to drink."

"And when we returned from our honeymoon," Morgan reminded him.

Color rushed up the back of his neck. "Yeah, well, no excuse there. I was caught in the throes of hormones, I guess. So," he gave her his full attention, "how have you been doin'?"

Morgan suspected the question had been right around the corner. She shifted on the bench and directed her gaze across the town square. "Just fine."

"A trained lie." Don chuckled. "Listen, I was wondering, while you're here, maybe you'd like to get together sometime. Nothing serious. Just dinner and a movie."

Morgan didn't have a chance to let him down easily for Evan jogged back across the manicured lawn, a stony look on his face. Nerves brought her to her feet. "What is it?"

He snagged her wrist. "We have to go. Don, talk to you later." Tugging her along behind him, Evan led the way back to his truck.

Morgan didn't try to make conversation until they'd both settled themselves in the cab of Evan's truck. She fastened her seatbelt and the second Evan started the engine, she began the questions. "What's wrong?"

He clamped the blue globe light on top of his dash. "I don't want you to panic."

Her eyes captured the fluorescent slivers of blue and white. "You should have told me that before you put the light up there. What's going on?"

"Your parents just got a call."

Morgan's blood ran cold. A sick feeling settled in the pit of her stomach. Surely, the bastard wouldn't come after her parents. He didn't know them...did he? And would it make a difference to Dexter Canfield even if he didn't know his victims? She clasped her hands together in her lap and fought for the control she could so easily acquire in the courtroom. It eluded her.

"Was it Dexter?" Her voice shook in time with her body and her nails dug into her palms.

"We don't know yet. Chadwick took the call from your dad."

"Dad would have called me." Morgan doubted the truth behind the words even as she said them. Jack Tanner wouldn't risk alarming his only daughter. He'd spent his life protecting her and he wouldn't change now. Especially now.

Evan didn't respond to the statement. Instead, he chose a different track. "I'm going to suggest that your parents take a vacation for a while."

Morgan began to perspire. "Mom won't leave the bakery."

"She can close it for a few days."

"She won't do that." Morgan hesitated. "Do you really think it'll only take a couple of days to catch Dexter?"

Evan turned a right corner too fast. The tires squealed and she held on to the hold overhead. "I don't know what to think. I'm just saying it might be safer for your parents."

"It might be safer for everyone if I get out of town."

"He'd hunt you down."

Morgan's chest tightened. "Thanks for that."

"You said you always expected honesty from me. I'm not going to change now, no matter how difficult it is to hear."

She looked at his profile. His strong features reassured her. Evan had always been able to take any situation and turn it around for the better, not counting their marriage. Nothing could have saved that. She reached across and touched his thigh. "You do realize there are some things you just can't fix, don't you?"

"If you believed that, you wouldn't have come back." Evan jammed on the brakes and jarred the truck to a stop in the Tanners' driveway. Then, releasing the catch on his seatbelt, he shifted to face her. "Look at me, Morgan." He waited until her eyes fixed on his face before continuing. "Whatever you hear in there, I need you to remain calm." He palmed her cheek. "I know this is difficult and if Dexter has made contact with your parents, it's going to be horrifying, but he wants to scare the hell out of you and everyone around you. Fear can be a powerful motivator, but he thinks, in you, fear will cripple. Don't allow it."

Morgan allowed the pep talk to sink in for a few moments before she nodded and unfastened her own seatbelt. "Okay. I'm ready."

Evan cupped her chin. "That's my girl." He winked and dropped his hand. "Just remember you're not alone this time."

Morgan's smile froze in place and she climbed out of the truck, still wearing it when she opened the front door of her parents' home.

The Tanners sat together on the living room sofa, Jack with one arm wrapped around his wife for support. They didn't rise when Evan and Morgan entered.

Evan tucked his sunglasses in the front of his shirt and sat across from them. "Who called?"

Jack looked more shaken than Morgan had ever seen, but when he spoke, his voice still rang with authority. "I'm not sure. Could have been that bastard, but I've never heard his voice before."

"Did you tape it, Dad?" Morgan sat on the edge of the sofa next to her father's knee.

Jack tapped her leg. "Of course I did, but I don't want you listening to it. It'll only make things worse for you."

Morgan sent Evan a look and he seemed to read her mind. His next words confirmed it. "Jack, Morgan's the only one who can identify his voice."

Jack surged to his feet. "She's not going to listen to it, I tell you!"

Diane stood beside her husband and hooked her arm through his. "Jack, Evan knows what he's doing."

Morgan got up and walked around behind the couch. "I'll be back in a second."

"Morgan, don't!" Jack called out after her, but Morgan didn't stop. She knew her mission.

To spare her parents, she closed the door behind her and walked across the kitchen floor. The phone hung on the wall next to her mother's wall calendar. She took several deep breaths, waiting for that surge of confidence she so desperately needed.

The door behind her opened and Evan walked in, a different form of confidence. He rested his hands on her shoulders. "Are you up to this?"

She leaned back against him for a moment. "You didn't ask me that when you told me about the call and yet, you knew I'd have to listen to the tape."

Evan wrapped his arms around her. "But it doesn't have to be right now. If you need more time, I'll understand."

She blew out a breath. "No. It has to be now. You and I both know every second we wait is a second that bastard gains on us." She reached out and depressed the play button, for once grateful her father had never given in to her demands for voice mail. At least now, Evan could listen with her.

"Hi. I'm trying to locate a friend of mine, Morgan Tanner Hennessy. I'm sure you know how I can find her, so if you wouldn't mind giving me a call." Long pause. "Or better yet, I'll just swing by. Yeah, that'll be even better. I think I'd like surprising her. If you could just tell Morgan I'll be there in a few days, I'd greatly appreciate it. Thanks." The call ended, and Morgan reached for Evan's hand.

"It was him," she breathed.

Evan turned her in his arms and held her tight for a long, silent moment. "We figured this was going to happen. He's just telling us what we already knew."

Morgan managed a nod to acknowledge his reassuring words. "Right."

Releasing her gently, Evan popped the tape out. "I'm taking this back to town with me. We need all the evidence we can get against this bastard. Now, why don't you go upstairs and pack a few things?"

"I can't leave them now, Evan."

He surprised her by kissing her, more a stamp of dominance than a glimpse at his passionate nature. "Morgan, go pack. I'll go talk to your parents."

She stood her ground. "I'm not leaving my parents to fend for themselves. I brought this monster here."

"He's not here yet and I'm not going to take chances with your life. So you can either come with your stuff or without it, but either way, you're coming with me, even if I have to arrest you."

Her mouth fell open. "Arrest me? You can't arrest me! I haven't done anything wrong."

He sauntered toward the door. "Maybe not yet, but by the time I write up the paperwork, I'll have thought of something. As of now, you're in police custody, baby."

Chapter Seven

Dexter dumped the remaining dregs of the cold coffee out the window and tossed the crumpled foam cup onto the passenger floor. He cranked up the music, a rowdy classic rock beat, and began the search for a hotel. His muscles ached from sitting so long and he needed time for a quick shower and some sleep before he greeted Morgan again. He had to be at his best when he met her family, too.

Whistling in time to the music, he accelerated onto the exit ramp, ignoring the posted speed limit. He came to a stop sign, the flickering lights of a vacancy sign capturing his attention. One seedy motel coming up. The perfect place to hide for the evening.

As he shot through the intersection, a siren whooped behind him. Dexter didn't bother to check the speedometer. He doubted the speed limit was much past "mosey" in this part of the country. He pulled the Navigator to the side of the road and clicked on the overhead light.

"Buddy, you're about to have a bad day." He chuckled and drew out a small flask of eighty-proof whiskey. "Yeah, this is one time, you should have gone home early to the missus." With the alcohol swirling around in his mouth, he flicked the lighter casually, his fascination with the flame momentarily distracting him.

The police officer arrived at the window, flicking a small flashlight into the driver's side window. The sudden beam annoyed Dexter and he recoiled.

"Could I see your driver's license and registration, please?"

Dexter continued to flick the flame while the whiskey scorched his tongue.

The officer released the catch on his weapon. "I said, driver's license and registration, please."

For a brief moment, Dexter heard his father's voice, that same booming bass which always accompanied a stinging slap to the back of the head. Always demanding, never giving an inch, the older Canfield had been the bane of Dexter's existence for eighteen years...until Dexter discovered the many beneficial uses of a cigarette lighter.

"Sir, I'm not going to ask you again." Was it his imagination or did the cop's voice shake?

Dexter spared the young officer a glance. A rookie. It figured. He couldn't get a challenge in today's world, it seemed. He turned his head ever so slightly, saw the fine, upstanding member of law enforcement withdraw his weapon and then, Dexter held the flame close to his lips and spat.

The whiskey ignited, sending an explosion of orange and blue flames cascading out the window and straight into the police officer's face. The cop howled and staggered back, smacking against the pain.

Dexter climbed out of the front seat and knelt down beside the screaming officer. "You should have called in sick today." He slipped a small penknife from the front pocket of his jeans and with quick, efficient moves, silenced the man's cries for help with a neat slice across the throat.

He straightened, patted his hair back into place and returned to the driver's seat. "I'm really unhappy about having to go to the next town for my sleep, but, well, I guess it can't be helped can it, Officer?" He stared down at the body for a long moment, while his father's own cries rang in his ears. The day he'd killed his old man was the day he'd been liberated.

"Let freedom ring," he sing-songed, turning the radio up full blast as he sped off into the night.

Morgan dumped her overnight bag onto the polished wooden floor just inside the entranceway. Evan didn't need to turn around to know she was angry, but he'd rather have her safe with him and furious than an open target.

"I have plenty of guestrooms upstairs. I'll show you." He reached behind him for her bag, but she barred his path.

"This isn't right, Evan."

"Do we have to keep killing the horse, Morgan? I'm doing this because..."

She held up one hand to silence him. "I'm not talking about being here right now. I'm talking about the phone call. We don't know how close Dexter is. He could be anywhere right now, even outside their window. What if...?"

Evan reached around her and snatched up the bag. "I've already planned for that contingency." He looked into her wary eyes. "Just because I'm a small-town sheriff doesn't mean I've forgotten my big city ways. Deputy Chadwick is going to sit on the house tonight and keep an eye out. If anyone shows up, he'll become a guest of Skyler's jail."

He watched her shoulders relax marginally. "Thank you."

Evan found himself growing irritated. He didn't want her gratitude. He tromped ahead of her. "Why don't you take a bath, get comfortable, while I fix us some dinner? I can't promise you fine cuisine, but I think my cooking skills have greatly improved since our divorce."

"Evan."

He stopped walking, one foot on the bottom step of the spiral staircase. "Yeah?" He didn't look back. He couldn't. Seeing her face right now would only send the blood rushing from his head and he needed to think clearly.

"I was being serious when I said thank you."

His hand curled around the banister. "I'm sure you were." He heard her soft footsteps behind him.

"Why are you angry?"

He gritted his teeth. Why did she feel the need to push the matter? Because she was Morgan and that's what Morgan did. She'd done it their entire marriage. Apparently, some things never changed. "Who said I was angry?"

"You always avoid answering my questions when you're angry."

He dropped the bag and turned. "Could we just not talk about this right now? I want to get through this night and—"

"You're regretting bringing me here," she surmised with all the accuracy of an arrow hitting a bull's-eye dead center.

He raked one hand through his hair and dropped down to sit on the wooden stairs. "No. Yes. Hell, I don't know what I'm thinking right now."

She came forward, even closer than before. If Evan lifted his eyes, he could see her slender waist, the zipper on her jeans. He managed to resist the urge, until she reached out to touch him. The second her hand made contact with his, his gaze shot upwards, over denim and locking on her face. "Evan, I can leave."

He turned his hand over on the banister and captured her fingers. "I don't want you to leave, Morgan. You need to be here. You'll be safe."

She leaned down and pressed her lips to his cheek. Evan jerked back. She straightened at once. "I'm sorry. I only meant to..."

He launched himself to his feet. "Yeah, I know. Thank me. You only wanted to thank me."

Morgan clutched at the sleeve of his shirt as he tried to walk away from her. "What's wrong with you? You're acting strange."

He came down the steps until he could stand face to face with her, body to body, his chest brushing hers. "Do you have any idea how beautiful you are right now?"

She blinked up at him. "What brought that on?" Her tongue flicked out to moisten her lips.

Evan smiled a little. He'd made her nervous. "You're just as beautiful now as you were the day I married you."

She lowered her head and her shoulders hunched. "You can't see all of me, Evan. There are parts of me you wouldn't think are beautiful."

He tucked her hair behind her ears and raised her face with gentle hands. "That could never happen." His fingers inched around behind her neck, working to loosen the knotted muscles.

Her hands clamped around his wrists. "You don't want to see this."

He dipped his head and kissed her. She tasted the same, that intoxicating blend of honey and fire. Heat engulfed him and the need to take her in his arms battered him. He gave into the desire, holding her like fragile glass against his chest. "Morgan,

I want to see all of you and not to prove anything to you." He stroked her hair. "I've missed holding you like this."

She shuddered. "It's been a long time since I've felt this safe."

The words tangled in his soul and Evan knew he had to put a stop to the moment. He wouldn't rush her, but he knew the time would come when the desire between them would overcome the past. He still wanted Morgan and no amount of time or distance would ever change that. He kissed the top of her head and separated their bodies. "Go take that bath. You need to eat." He kissed her cheek, her eyelids and then her lips again to reassure her.

Morgan began to back up the stairs, confusion swirling within the depths of her green eyes. Evan waited until he heard the water running overhead before he slipped into his office and closed the door.

He made one phone call, and the network he'd left behind in New York came to life. The FBI agents with combined centuries on the job immediately stepped up to the plate. With more technology at their fingertips than Skyler, North Carolina would see in the next forty years, the agents would track Dexter Canfield and in spite of regulations, pass the information onto Evan.

He gave them sketchy details, all he had, but the agents were no less willing to help, including one colleague in particular Evan had always clashed with, because when it came down to the wire, the good always stood with each other.

"So you think this asshole's on his way then?"

Evan heard the growl in Dutch Baker's voice. Dutch came across as a gritty, take no prisoners type of FBI agent, but Evan knew he had a heart of gold and would stop at nothing to help his friends.

Evan glanced at the door and lowered his voice. "Without a doubt. He's not stopping."

Dutch cursed and Evan heard his boots thump against the floor of his deck. Living in Staten Island, Dutch chose to retain a portion of his country roots and had moved his family to a modified cabin with most of the luxuries of the city, but none of the hassles, like traffic and crowded grocery stores.

"Well, you know I'll do what I can. I'll check the wire and if anything comes across, you'll be the first to know. And if you need any of us to come, you know I got your back."

Evan relaxed only marginally. "Thanks. I knew I could count on you guys."

Dutch cleared his throat. "So how's Morgan holding up?"

Evan's grip on the cordless tightened. "She's changed, Dutch."

"You mean because of the fire?"

"Not just that."

"Bastard," Dutch ground out. "Yeah, well, we'll get him. No doubt about that." Long pause. "Does Morgan know you called us?"

"No, but she will. I'll tell her tonight. I'm sure she'll appreciate the help."

"You seeing her tonight then?"

"She's here." Evan knew the second he said the words Dutch would let the matter drop. He'd never been one to pry and he was a firm believer in minding his own business.

Dutch expelled an audible breath. "Well, take it easy, buddy. You've got the Federal Bureau behind you and nothing can stop the FBI."

Evan laughed a little at the old joke before he rang off. He sat holding the phone for a long time, playing the conversation and the events of his history over in his head. He'd known he could depend upon the friends he'd made in New York. They'd been a tight-knit group and with Dutch, Ace, Crowder and Iggy working behind the scenes, Evan knew the odds in favor of catching Dexter Canfield just tripled.

But he wouldn't rest easier until he'd put a bullet between Canfield's eyes.

He didn't especially care for the motel, but as Dexter checked in using fake identification, he noticed the blonde with killer legs, pointy breasts and a short, tight skirt. Perhaps the motel had possibilities.

As he hoisted the small bag holding exactly one change of clothes, a toothbrush and a razor, he strolled away from the desk, pausing to pretend to inspect the stack of magazines strewn out across the coffee table with three legs and a stack of wood for the missing fourth.

From the corner of his eye, he saw the blonde watching him with interest. She wore too much make-up for his tastes, but it had been a while since he'd enjoyed the pleasures of the flesh. He figured he could lower his standards for one evening.

He lifted his head and noticed the woman had shifted on the flowered loveseat. She now sat with one leg cocked high, giving Dexter an unobstructed view of her attributes.

Perfect. He couldn't have planned this better himself. He must be the luckiest son-of-a-bitch in the world. Who knew hookers worked in Podunkville, too?

Chapter Eight

Morgan sank into the frothy bubbles and as the steamy water penetrated her aching muscles, she gave a sigh of relief. She couldn't remember the last time she'd tucked her fears away and just enjoyed the pleasures of the moment. Now, with Evan downstairs, she felt safe, protected.

The warmth soothed away the aches and pains and allowed the tension to drift away much as the steam did underneath the door. The oval mirror atop the vanity fogged and wet tendrils of hair clung to the sides of her face. Morgan felt herself sinking into oblivion.

She adjusted her position and the grotesque scars on her left arm slipped from beneath the bubbles. She quickly closed her eyes. She didn't want to see the ugliness. She didn't need the reminder. For now, even if just for a few minutes, she wanted to pretend she was the other Morgan, the one Evan had married so many years ago, that same, perfect woman.

She heard the tap on the bathroom door before Evan called her name. "Morgan?"

Her heart began to pound against her chest and she prayed he wouldn't open the door. "I'll be out in a second." Someone wasn't listening to her prayers for the door opened. Frantically, she ducked beneath the cloak of water. "I said I'd be out in a minute." Her voice sounded shrill even to her own ears.

Evan kept his eyes averted. "Sorry. I didn't hear you. You forgot the towels." He placed a stack of fluffy, white towels on the vanity stool and began to back from the bathroom.

From her vantage point, she could see the way his well-worn jeans clung to his impressive thighs. She remembered too well the feeling of power in those muscles. Desperate to take her mind off the erotic images, she blurted out. "This looks like a woman's bathroom." Morgan regretted the comment, but it was too late to retract it.

Evan paused by the door. "Yeah, I know. My sister thought I needed at least one room a female could feel comfortable in." His lips twitched. "Although she never told me why."

"I didn't mean to sound, well, accusing."

He looked at her then and Morgan found herself wanting to sink as close to the bottom of the claw-footed tub as the porcelain would allow. "There's been no other woman here, Morgan."

Her heart skipped a beat before resuming its normal rhythm. "Well, it's none of my business anyway." She fiddled with the smooth edge of the tub, hoping he'd go away and when she peeked up and saw that was his intention, regret coursed through her.

Evan turned back toward the door. "It's always been your business." He tossed her a glance over his shoulder. "And it always will be."

Once he closed the door behind him, Morgan stared at the wood. She didn't want to decipher what he meant by the enigmatic words. But that part of her feminine nature buried deep inside her since the attack began to stir. Evan could always entice that elemental part of her soul. Now, being here, this close to him, she felt the same magic she'd left behind.

She didn't need to ask herself what it was about the man that made her insides dance. He was strong, powerful, charming and could make any woman glad she was born with that certain chromosome. And in spite of everything she'd endured over the past few months, she was glad. Glad to be back.

Glad to be home.

"You ain't paid me yet."

If the bitch whined again, he'd have to kill her. Dexter flopped onto his back and draped his arm across his eyes. Of course, he wanted to wait until he was up to giving her one more go around first.

She poked him in the ribs. "Are you listening to me?" The flimsy mattress creaked beneath her slight weight as she jostled herself into a better position to peer down into his face.

His arm slipped a notch and he caught her beady eyes staring down at him. He resisted the urge to swat her. "I heard you. You'll get paid."

"I like to be paid up front. If that's not something you're going to do, well, then, I reckon I'd better make myself scarce." She rolled toward the edge of the bed, but Dexter snagged her arm. His nails dug into her flesh and the swift intake of her breath pleased him. "Ow! You're hurting me!" She tried to wrench her arm free, but he hauled her back down onto the bed. "Let go of me!"

Dexter wrapped his hand around her neck and brought her face close to his. "I've had just about enough of your bitching, so shut up. Do you hear me?" He raised his voice to make sure. At the hooker's fearful nod, he relaxed somewhat. "Good." He released his hand and patted her cheek. "Now, we're going to have a good time here tonight, and when it's over, I'll pay you everything I owe you, and if you're good to me," he winked, "I'll even tip you."

The blonde shrank back against the pillow on her side of the bed and blinked at him. "You hadn't told me your name."

Dexter's lips curled. "You don't need to know my name. I like it that way. I didn't ask yours, either."

"It's Sheila," she said in a meek tone of voice.

"I didn't want to know that." He turned his head on his pillow and fixed her with a studious look. "But you look like a Sheila. Knew a Sheila once in high school. Smart little bitch, she was. Didn't like me at all." His eyes drifted to the right as the memories swept over him. "At least not at first, but in the end," he chuckled, "she liked me just fine." He rubbed his hand up and down Sheila's thigh. "You like me, don't you, Sheila?"

"Sure, I do." The words sounded false, but Dexter accepted them anyway.

"Good. That's real good. I think you'll get that tip."

Morgan buried her shoulders in the scented water. The heat soothed her, massaging the scars. She closed her eyes and rested her head against the foam pillow behind her. If she tried hard enough, she could almost forget the horrors of the past few months.

"Morgan." Evan tapped at the bathroom door and cracked it open. "I forgot to tell you there's shaving cream under the cabinet if you need it."

The little reminder made her smile. During their marriage, she'd used his shaving cream instead of her own because she liked the scent. It had reminded her of him. "You can come in," she whispered. Butterflies began to dance in her stomach. She had no reason to be nervous around Evan and yet, her muscles tensed as the doorknob turned.

As if given permission to enter the queen's quarters, Evan walked inside hesitantly, keeping his eyes averted.

Suddenly, she had to ask. "Evan?"

He stopped. "Yeah?"

"Why did you tell me I'm beautiful?"

He spun around then, his brows furrowed. "What kind of question is that?"

She kept her eyes lowered. She didn't want to see the pity in his eyes, wasn't even sure that's what she would see, but she didn't think she could bear reading the sympathy on Evan's face. She needed honesty from him, but irrationally, she wanted it coated in sugar. "One I'd like an answer to."

"I told you that because it's the truth."

She lifted her arm out of the bubbles and extended it overhead. The bubbles fell away from the ugly, twisted skin and for a moment, however brief, she thought about hiding again. But desperation made her hold strong. "Even with these?" She surprised herself by baring the scars to Evan's line of view, but hurt curled within the pit of her stomach. She'd showed no one all the hideous reminders of Dexter's attack, at least not voluntarily. "Do you still think I'm beautiful with these?" Her arm shook a bit, but she refused to lower it, not until she knew for sure.

Evan took two steps toward her and stopped. He looked down into her upturned face and for a brief moment, Morgan saw a flash of uncertainty in his eyes. She wanted to retract the statement, but mostly, she wanted to sink down into the water, hiding herself from the stark pain she saw hidden within the depths of those hazel orbs.

"Don't answer that," she instructed. "That was just me feeling sorry for myself." She tucked her arm back into the froth and slipped down until her chin touched the water. "I would have asked for the cream if I'd needed it."

Instead of taking the hint and leaving, Evan knelt down beside the tub. He draped one hand over the porcelain edge and trailed his fingers in the water. The ripples tickled her chin. "I know, but it was the only excuse I could think of to come back in here with you."

She nodded, the water brushing her lips. "I thought as much."

"I'm going to answer your question anyway, Morgan."

Panic made her protest. She wished she'd never brought it up. She should have remembered Evan wasn't one to drop a topic. "There's no need."

He didn't look up, but his voice reached her loud and strong. "You will always be beautiful." He scooped up a swatch of bubbles and held them in his palm. "Scars can't change that. I know who you are on the inside." He blew the foam from his hand. "Don't ever doubt that, Morgan." His hand dove beneath the water and she felt his fingers move over the thick skin. "You still take my breath away."

Tears caused her throat to swell. Evan always had the gift of words. She touched his hand. "Thank you."

He looked at her then. Their eyes met, clung and he smiled. "One day, you're going to show me every one of those scars."

Her heart began to thud, beating louder and louder in her ears. "I wouldn't be too sure of that."

He touched the tip of his finger to her nose. "Oh, I'm absolutely positive."

She frowned, trying to see past the smug look on his face. "Care to share how you know?"

He grinned and straightened, stretching his arms over his head. "Eventually, you'll give in to the desire to fall into my arms again. You've never been able to resist me."

Morgan shook her head and splashed her hand against the water, spraying Evan's neatly pressed white shirt. He laughed and staggered back. Then, with his eyes intent on her face, he approached the pedestal sink.

"What are you doing?" She sat up straighter in the tub, peering upwards. She couldn't see around his broad shoulders. "Evan?" She heard the water running and when Evan turned, with a clear cup full of water, she squealed.

"Don't! Don't you dare, Evan! I swear to God, you'll regret it." She swiveled in the tub, but Evan approached with a wicked gleam in his eye.

"You know the saying, if you can't run with the big dogs..." He didn't finish the cliché.

Morgan held her hands up to ward off an attack, bringing her breasts into full view. Evan lowered the cup a fraction of an inch. Her gaze dropped for an instant before lifting. She sent her ex-husband a disgusted look. "You're easily distracted."

He gave her an unabashed shrug. "I'm a man."

"I've never questioned that." She kept one eye on the cup of water while she lowered her voice, using her most sultry tones.

"No?" He took another step closer.

She shook her head and trailed one damp finger around her lips. "Never."

Evan heaved a dramatic sigh. "Well, I appreciate that. I also appreciate the college try, but," he raised the cup and dumped the water over her head, "no accolades."

Morgan spluttered and shivered as the cool liquid soaked her head and rained down onto her exposed breasts. "Dammit, Evan." She brushed her sopping hair away from her eyes and saw him kneeling down beside the tub. She glared at him. "Don't even think about it."

He cupped the back of her head. "All I've done is think about it." His lips touched hers and heat exploded like a starburst in the center of her stomach. Their breaths mingled in the fogginess of the air and Morgan leaned into the kiss, her hands clutching the material of his shirt.

Evan dragged her into a world of memories, exploring territory he had to remember as well as she did. His tongue traced her lips before dueling with hers. She came to her knees in the tub and wrapped her arms around his neck, giving herself to the spiraling passions.

Evan's hands stroked her back, her sides and then, with a violent move, Morgan pushed away from him, diving back underneath the shelter of the water. Droplets of water clung to his hair and confusion swirled in his eyes. "What was that all about?" He touched two fingers to his lips.

Morgan covered her breasts with her hands. "Nothing. Never mind. It shouldn't have happened."

He surveyed her for a long moment before climbing to his feet. "It's because I touched you."

"You didn't touch me. You touched the scars."

"The scars are part of you."

"Thank you, Dr. Hennessy. Now, I'd like to finish my bath."

He walked to the sink and gripped the edge of the porcelain. "Hiding from this won't make it go away, Morgan."

"Evan, please. I don't want to discuss this."

"You don't want to discuss this with anyone or just me?"

"Does it matter?"

Two long strides carried him to the door. "Hell, yes, it matters. You used to be able to tell me anything."

Morgan lowered her gaze and tried to focus on the dissipating bubbles. "We used to be married."

The slamming of the bathroom door signaled his departure.

She sank lower into the cooling water and tried not to cry. She couldn't explain the desperate need to push Evan away, but then, she didn't want to try. The woman Evan married years ago didn't exist anymore. He wouldn't understand that. He needed her to be Morgan Tanner, his childhood sweetheart, the same innocent girl with big dreams and even bigger goals.

Morgan swiped at the tears on her cheeks. That girl became a woman and the strongest part of that woman died when the fire scorched her skin.

Evan sank down into the cushions of the sofa and twisted the top off the beer. He'd checked in with the station and Chadwick assured him all was quiet. Evan wouldn't be needed tonight...at least not by the citizens of Skyler. He flicked a glance toward the spiral staircase. Whether she would admit it or not, Morgan needed him. And that was precisely the reason why she came home.

He stared at the framed picture adorning the mantle of his fireplace. Morgan in her wedding gown, her face flushed, eyes glowing. He wore a rented tuxedo and a smile that had caused his jaws to ache by the end of the night. He hadn't cared. He'd just married his best friend, the woman he wanted to spend the rest of his life with. He still didn't quite understand where everything went wrong.

He thought their marriage was normal. They'd made compromises, adjustments to the everyday life of living together.

He loved her. Desperately. The day she walked out, he'd cracked. He would never admit that to anyone, but his buddies at the department had known. They'd covered for him as long as they could until Evan had taken an extended leave of absence from the force. Extended leave segued into the job as Skyler's sheriff.

In retrospect, he suspected he'd returned to his hometown simply because it contained more memories of Morgan than New York had. He'd needed those memories to recover and he'd started the healing process, until Morgan showed back up.

"Evan?" She called him from the top of the stairs.

He sat up straight and looked up. She stood wrapped in his white, terry robe, her face scrubbed clean of make-up and her hair piled on top of her head in a haphazard bun. Evan couldn't take his eyes off of her.

"Evan?" Uncertain, she began to descend the stairs.

He stood and walked toward her. "You look like you feel better." He'd wanted to say stunning, gorgeous, absolutely breathtaking, but the wariness in her eyes made him keep those descriptions to himself.

He saw her shoulders relax and she continued her descent. "I do. Thank you."

He took hold of her arm and walked her to the sofa. Her gratitude was starting to grate on his nerves, but he kept that to himself, too. "Do you want a glass of wine? A pink lady?"

Morgan smiled and shook her head. "No, I'm fine, but finish your beer. I didn't mean to interrupt."

He sat back down and patted the cushion beside him. "You can't interrupt memories."

She sat, folding her hands in her lap. "I'm sorry."

"For what?" He gave her the opening, allowing her to take the lead.

"For snapping at you, for reacting so strongly upstairs."

He scratched her back with light, gentle strokes. "Morgan, I can't begin to understand what you've gone through, what this recovery process has done to you. You don't need to apologize to me. Sure, you pissed me off, but it's not like you've never done that before." He flashed her a grin. "I'm sure I've returned the favor on many occasions."

She leaned back, sandwiching his hand against the sofa. "Are you sure it's a good idea for me to be here?"

"Where else would you be?"

"My parents are probably scared to death."

"Chadwick is going to make runs by their house every hour. He'll keep a watch on them."

"You don't have the manpower for that."

"You let me worry about the manpower. Besides, ever since you arrived, people are coming out of the woodwork wanting to volunteer. Everyone cares about you here."

She tipped her head back to see his face. "I know. That was always one of the nice things about Skyler."

"I also called Dutch and the gang."

Morgan stiffened noticeably. "Are they coming here?"

"No, but they can give me a helluva lot of information I couldn't get any other way. If Canfield is within sniffing distance of the Skyler town limits, I'll know." He patted her knee. "Hell, I'll know when he's within one hundred miles of here. Those fellas are that good."

"You don't need to tell me that, Evan. They are a good group of guys."

"But you never cared for them."

111

"I never cared for the type of danger they put you in. They used you one too many times."

"I went undercover willingly, Morgan. I was a cop. It was what I wanted to do."

"The FBI had men for that, and these friends of yours knew you were married. They put your life on the line and didn't give a damn if you didn't come home." She turned his hand over on her knee and stroked the inside of his palm like she used to do when they were settled in for the evening in front a roaring fire.

"Well, you don't have to worry about any of this now. The only crime Skyler sees is an occasional drunk and disorderly."

Morgan released a breath and slipped down lower, nestling her head on his shoulder. She yawned and Evan felt her body relaxing against his, succumbing to the call of sleep.

"You must be exhausted. Do you want to go to bed?"

Her head lifted and her eyes, those vivid green orbs which could see through to his soul, fixed on his face. "Is that an invitation?"

Every muscle in his body knotted. "No, but it can be."

She laughed a little and touched his cheek. "I don't think you know what you're getting yourself into."

His brows drew together. "What are you talking about?"

"I'm not the same woman you married, Evan."

"That I already know."

"I don't know if I can ever be that woman again."

He drew her head down to his chest and held her with his palm pressed against her cheek. "You don't have to be the same woman. You just go on from here. Everyone changes. That's not necessarily a bad thing."

"Didn't you hate me?"

The thought was laughable. Hate had never entered his vocabulary when it came to Morgan. Sure, she could piss him off like no other woman and occasionally, she could irritate the hell out of him. But she could always make him melt inside with just a smile. Or the gentle whisper of his name.

"Evan?" Morgan waved a hand in front of his face. "You didn't answer me."

"That's because I thought we'd discussed this. We both knew it was a matter of time before one of us walked out."

"I hurt you," she whispered.

"I'm sure I did the same to you." He kissed the top of her head. He was sure she'd spent a lot of time blaming herself about the break-up of their marriage, but if the truth were told, he was probably more to blame. Spending so many long hours away from her while he was undercover, forcing her to live with the anxiety of waiting for that phone call in the middle of the night, and then forgetting everything from her birthday to their anniversary.

Yeah, he figured he was more than fifty percent to blame.

She shifted in his arms and pressed a kiss against his neck. Evan's blood surged lower. Morgan snuggled closer to his chest, one leg draping over his knee.

"Morgan." He said her name on a warning.

"I want to show you something." She pulled away from him and Evan clenched his hands into fists. He couldn't decipher the look in her eyes, but the second she released the tie on the robe, he understood. He caught hold of her wrist.

"You don't have to do this."

She smiled, though it didn't reach her eyes. "If I can't show my scars to you, who can I show them to, Evan? You've been my best friend for over twenty-five years. You know everything about me and even though our marriage was a mistake, we've never stopped loving each other."

Her words sent a dagger into his heart. She'd said them before. They'd hurt then, too. He couldn't keep the anger from his voice. "I never considered our marriage a mistake."

Her face softened. "No, you're right. It was more of a learning process." She slipped the robe from her shoulders and Evan saw the stretch of puckered skin beginning at her collarbone. "You caught just a glimpse of it when you came to pick me up for my doctor's appointment, but this is all of it."

She withdrew her arm from the terry cloth and laid it atop Evan's leg. The skin covering the shoulder bore the marks of Canfield's cruelty. Red and twisted, it ran the length from her shoulder to just past her elbow. Morgan stood to allow the robe to drop to the floor. Standing before him naked, she pivoted, giving Evan a full view of the damage the fire caused.

Instead of focusing on the scars, Evan shifted his attention to Morgan's face. He saw the fine sheen of tears in her eyes and the nervousness she couldn't hide. He gave her a slow, reassuring smile before he allowed his gaze to travel over her wounds. He took in every graft, every inch of the excruciating transformation.

Then he stood and held out his hands. When Morgan took hold, he drew her closer, meshing her body against his. "I don't know what you wanted me to see, Morgan, but I'll tell you what I did see. I saw a beautiful, desirable woman with more courage and strength than ten women." He cupped her face and looked into her teary eyes. "I still see the woman I fell in love with. Scars don't change who you are on the inside, except to draw out the tenacity and spirit you've had all along." He kissed her and tasted the salt of her tears. "Now, I'm standing here with a naked woman in my arms and I find myself not interested in talking any longer."

Morgan laughed against his lips and when his hands slipped around her waist, she didn't tense. Instead, she stood on tiptoe and deepened the kiss while her hands clutched his shirt.

His sex responded with a violent surge and Evan mentally restrained himself. He had to slow down. Gentling his hands, he ended the kiss and touched his forehead to hers. "What do you want tonight, Morgan? Answer me honestly."

"I don't want to think anymore, Evan. I want to forget everything that's happened, at least for a few hours. I want to fall asleep in your arms and wake up the way I used to." She gave him a watery smile. "It sounds like I want to use you."

He grinned a little. "I wouldn't object to being used."

"Will you make love to me?"

He couldn't imagine any sweeter words and while instincts told him to seize the moment, his conscience told him it wasn't what Morgan needed. He reached for the self-control which had slipped away somewhere after Morgan dropped the robe. "As much as I'd love to make love to you tonight, I think you need a night without demands even more." He scooped her up into his arms before she could protest. "So I am taking you to bed, Mrs. Hennessy, but only to hold you while you sleep. When you wake up, I'll still be holding you and," he kissed her with a slight brush of his lips, "you'll know you really are safe."

Morgan dropped her head to his shoulder. "Well, it's not my first choice, but I guess it will have to do."

He carried her up the stairs. "It's nice to know it wasn't your first choice."

Chapter Nine

"Crazy son-of-a-bitch," Sheila groused, flinging her tattered jean jacket around her shoulders before storming out of the motel room.

Dexter rolled to his back and stuck a cigarette in his mouth. He flicked his lighter and the smoke curled upwards toward the ceiling. He heard Sheila's heels clicking on the concrete, and he chortled. He'd scared the piss out of her with the lighter and his flask of alcohol, but he'd never seriously intended to kill her. He didn't kill non-essentials and hookers were non-essentials in his book.

He drew the nicotine deep into his lungs and sat up, propping the stack of pillows behind him. Sheila hadn't been half-bad, but he wished now that he'd continued on his journey to Skyler instead of taking the break. Every local station talked incessantly about the hurricane approaching the North Carolina coast and though Skyler was far enough inland, the projected path took the monster storm directly toward the small town, a move that would undoubtedly louse up his plans. Fire and torrential downpours didn't go together very well.

He increased the volume on the color television bolted to the wall. A voluptuous redhead standing in front of a map pointed toward the coastline and, in an excited voice, warned residents about the potential for flooding and isolated tornadoes. Dexter cursed and flopped back down against the mattress. He didn't have much time to put his plan into action. He'd have to act quickly.

He couldn't complete his mission without his lighter. Without fire.

The sun streamed into the room, its glare shining directly in Morgan's eyes. She tried to adjust her position, but a heavy arm across her waist prevented much movement. She cracked open one eyelid and saw Evan's unshaven jaw.

She contented herself with watching him, listening to him breathe and feeling the rough texture of his cheek against her palm. True to his word, he'd only held her the night before, making no other move. Though she'd lain naked in his arms, he simply enfolded her in his embrace. They'd chatted in the darkness, their conversation of no consequence, but the comfort the night brought to Morgan meant everything.

She smiled and brought her hand down to his throat, testing the corded muscles and then moving it even lower to his shoulder, the breadth of his chest. She'd always admired his toned abs and narrow waist. A runner, Evan kept in shape by jogging at least three miles a day. His lean build and athletic legs gave him plenty of stamina and Morgan had been the lucky recipient of all of that energy.

Her smile widened and she felt the heat rush to her cheeks. Their marriage hadn't lacked for sex and she'd certainly had no complaints. In fact, if they could have simply stayed in the bedroom all of their days, she probably never would have left.

"Why are you smiling?"

Evan's voice, husky with sleep, startled her and her heart jumped. She looked up and caught his drowsy, hazel eyes watching her.

She managed to adjust herself so that he couldn't see her face. "No reason. It was just nice to wake up like this."

He leaned closer to her, placing his lips next to her ear. "If your hand moves any lower, you're going to wake something else up."

Morgan didn't immediately remove her hand. Instead, she spread her fingers low on his abdomen. "Maybe I want to wake it up."

"Morgan." He closed his eyes and simply breathed.

She didn't resist the urge to touch him, to caress him and while Evan remained perfectly still, her hands recalled every glorious inch of her husband's body. Funny she couldn't think of him as her ex-husband at the present moment.

She tested his weight in her palm, stroking the taut skin and dragging low, vibrating moans from deep within his chest. "Apparently, I've created a monster," she whispered.

"You shouldn't be doing this." Evan managed to respond, though the words were broken.

"I've never followed the rules," she replied, continuing to taunt him with teasing fingertips and smooth brushes of her palm.

"I feel that."

"Is that a complaint?" She increased the pressure.

Evan groaned. "No. Definitely not a complaint."

She scooted lower on the mattress and bathed the tense muscles of his thighs with her tongue. Evan jerked and fisted his hands in her hair. He wouldn't stop her now. She'd taken him past the edge of reason.

Morgan braced her hands on either side of his hips and dipped her head. She hovered inches away from his sex, raising her head to see his face. "Do you want me to stop, Evan?" She felt powerful, strong, amazing. Evan had always made her feel this way.

His breath left his lungs on a burst of air. "That's not nice, Morgan."

She laughed and lowered her head. The shrill ring of the telephone jerked them both to attention. She sprang away from him, clutching her hands against her chest. She didn't speak and neither did Evan until he snatched the receiver from the cradle and barked his name.

He sat straight up in bed and Morgan crawled up beside him.

"When? How did it happen?"

Morgan knew by the tone of Evan's voice that Dexter had struck again. She didn't need Evan to tell her the details, but as the knowledge sank in, she climbed from the bed and padded to the bathroom. The conversation continued in muted tones, but she'd heard all she needed to hear.

Wrapping a towel around her body, she tucked the knot next to her breasts. She didn't pause to think about the scars fully visible in the light of day. All she needed right now were her clothes. Because she desperately needed to leave.

"What are you doing?" Evan stood in the doorway of the bathroom, the cordless in his hand.

Morgan fastened her eyes on her own reflection in the mirror. "You know, if I concentrate hard enough, I can still feel the flames."

"Morgan, for God's sake." Evan strode into the room and took hold of her shoulders. "You don't need to be thinking about things like that."

"Why? Because it's in the past? It's not in the past, Evan. That phone call was about Dexter, wasn't it? He killed someone else." Evan's silence gave her the answer she sought. Morgan twisted free of his hands and ducked beneath his arms to make it back into the bedroom. "He's not going to stop. He's just going to keep killing on a path to find me."

"You can't stop him from that, Morgan, and if you're thinking about trying to, rest assured I will not allow that."

She didn't have the energy to fight with him. She simply walked out of the bedroom.

Evan followed. "Dammit. Listen to me. Canfield is a psychotic bastard who chose you as the target of his attention. It could have been anyone else. You can't blame yourself for the other victims."

Morgan plowed through the overnight bag she'd brought with her and tugged a pair of jeans free from the tangle of her hairdryer cord. She slipped into a pair of lacy panties while Evan stood in the doorway. "I'm thinking about his upcoming victims, the people that live here in this town."

"So what is your plan then? You think sacrificing yourself is going to stop him?"

She stuffed her arms into a blue, cotton T-shirt and yanked it over her head. "No, I don't, but I'm not about to sit around waiting for that bastard to come back and finish the job." Her voice rose an octave and Evan simply folded his arms over his chest and waited for her to complete her thought. "I won't be a victim again."

"You want to tell me what's going through your head or do you want me to guess?"

She recognized the droll tone and for a brief second, she almost smiled. Evan used sarcasm liberally in their disagreements. Some things never changed. "I want you to teach me how to shoot a gun."

Evan straightened, his hands falling to his sides. "Are you kidding me? You've always hated guns!"

"That was then. This is now."

"Now, why didn't I think of that?" Evan stormed into the bedroom and yanked the hairbrush out of her hand. "You've had a consummate fear of guns your entire life and now that your own life is threatened, you want me to arm you? Now I know you're hysterical."

"Think what you want to think, Evan, but I need to be able to protect myself and my family."

"No, you don't. That's what I'm here for."

"You can't be with me all the time."

"Who says?"

"You weren't with me in Raleigh." The words sank in and Morgan saw the fury tighten Evan's jaw. She immediately recanted her words. "I didn't mean it the way it sounded."

He held up one hand. "You don't need to pacify me, Morgan. I know you're angry, hurt, bitter and many other adjectives, but that doesn't change my decision. I won't teach you how to fire a gun because quite frankly, I think the last thing you need is a dangerous weapon in your hands."

"And what if Dexter comes armed?"

Evan retreated to the doorway. "Then I'll be ready for him and you'll be tucked away safely inside while I deal with him."

"And what if he comes when you're not looking, Evan? When you're asleep."

"Will you stop? We don't live in what-if land! Whatever happens, I will deal with it."

Morgan snatched her hairbrush from the edge of the bed and marched toward him. "You'll deal with it? It's not just your life or the lives of the citizens in this town that we're talking about, Evan. It's my life. Mine. And I will damn well have a say in how I choose to protect myself."

His face took on a mutinous expression. "Well, good luck, because no one in this town will teach you how to shoot."

"Skyler has a firing range."

"I'm telling you, Morgan. No one here will help you. I can promise you that."

Morgan turned her back on him. "Just go away. If you don't want to help me, I'll find someone who will."

"I do want to help you and you won't find another living soul in this town who will go against my wishes."

Morgan snorted. "You're not that powerful, Evan."

"We'll see." He closed the door behind him.

Morgan turned and hurled the brush. It bounced off the wood, doing little to ease the pressure cooker of her emotions.

Evan dropped Morgan off at her mother's bakery and with a warning look, informed Mrs. Tanner that Morgan was to stay put until he returned for her. He ignored the blistering glares Morgan sent his way and sped toward the station.

Ian sat just inside the door, reading the morning paper and slurping a mug of coffee. "Morning, Sheriff."

Evan heard the smirk in the older man's voice, but chose to ignore it. "Good morning." He tried to make it past Ian's nosiness without success. He heard the rustle of the newspaper and knew Ian was moving in for the kill.

"Heard you spent the night with the former Mrs. Hennessy."

Evan stopped, one hand on the wooden swing gate separating the lobby from the offices. "Where did you hear that?" He looked over his shoulder.

Ian scrubbed his whiskers and shrugged, trying to look innocent. "Oh, you know, word gets around."

"You shouldn't listen to rumors, Ian."

"When you're retired, there ain't much else to do." He stood and stretched with a crackle of bones. "Take my word for it, Evan. You and Morgan will be remarried before the year is out."

"I don't have time for this."

"Well, if you expect me to believe you've only been spending time with her to protect her, you ain't right."

Evan turned around. "She asked me to teach her how to shoot." He didn't know what made him share the information, but now that the words were out, his shoulders relaxed. Ian would have an opinion; he always had one.

Ian shuffled forward. "You should." The response took Evan back long enough for the old man to continue. "If you don't teach her how to handle a gun and something happens, she'll never forgive you. We both know that ain't what you want."

Evan never figured the older man would actually have a point, but this time, he did. He rubbed his face with his palms. "She doesn't like guns."

"She doesn't know anything about them. You could teach her the right amount of respect for them."

"I don't have a lot of time."

Ian checked his watch. "No time like the present. Besides, the latest weather report says there's one mother of a storm system headed our way."

Evan shook his head, trying to keep up with the man's logic. "What does that have to do with anything?"

The older man sauntered toward the double glass doors. "Even if Morgan's attacker arrives, the rain's gonna hinder his fire-starting routine." He bobbed his head. "He might have to

123

come up with another game plan which gives you more time to help Morgan and plan your own attack." The former Marine shoved open the door. "Just remember to watch your back."

Evan watched him leave and amble down the sidewalk. Sometimes, he just couldn't quite figure Ian out. But this time, the man was making sense. As much as he didn't like the idea of arming Morgan, he'd have to teach her how to protect herself.

He'd just have to make sure she never had to use it.

"Your father and I think we should all leave town. You'll be safer, and we'll feel better knowing you're safe." Diane Tanner began the conversation after she enveloped Morgan in a flour-covered hug.

Morgan brushed the white spots off her T-shirt and dipped one finger in the bowl of icing on her mother's baking table. She wasn't surprised at her mother's need to save her. Always protective, always loving, Dianne Tanner had watched over Morgan like a hawk when she was growing up. "I'm not so sure that I can leave, Mom."

Diane clamped her hands on her hips and clicked her tongue. "Don't be ridiculous." She brushed her silver bangs away from her forehead with her wrist before shoving her hands into two thick potholders. "We watch the news, too, Morgan. Dexter Canfield is dangerous."

"You don't need to tell me that," Morgan said in a quiet voice.

Diane blew out a breath that caused her bangs to dance. "So it's settled then. We'll leave this afternoon."

Morgan placed her palms down on the aluminum baking table. "Mom, I can't leave."

"Yes, you can." Diane's voice hardened.

"But I think you and Dad should leave."

Diane opened the door of the brick oven and pulled out a loaf of fresh-baked bread. "Hand me that bundt cake." She stuffed the cake into the oven, closed the door and reset the timer. "And you know good and well your father and I won't go anywhere without you."

Morgan leaned across the table and covered her mother's mittened hand. "I appreciate what you're trying to do. I really do, but I can't run from Dexter. He'll only come after me."

"The police will catch him eventually."

"No, they won't, Mom. Dexter is too good."

"Then what makes you think you're safe here?"

"Because Evan is better." She slid off the stool and walked around to where her mother stood with a shaky expression on her face. "I trust him, Mom."

Diane busied her hands with cleaning up the table and situating the tools she needed to ice the cake. "You always did."

Morgan took hold of her mother's hand. "Then trust me to know I'm making the best decision for me."

Diane faced her daughter. "I can't leave you, Morgan. Your father won't, either." She cupped Morgan's face and more flour drifted to the front of Morgan's shirt. "You're our baby."

Morgan watched the tears fill her mother's eyes and she bit her lower lip to keep her own emotions in check. "This is going to turn out okay, Mom. I have to believe that. Dexter has taken enough of my life away. I won't let him take the rest."

Diane sighed and kissed Morgan on both cheeks. "I'll talk to your father again, but he's not going to be happy."

Morgan smiled and bumped her forehead to her mother's. "I would feel better if you and Dad would get out of town for a while."

Diane's hands dropped. "Out of the question."

Though she wanted to continue the conversation, Morgan knew it would be a lost cause. She'd gotten her stubbornness from her mother. With a sigh, she tucked her hair back behind her ears and walked to the serviceable black phone at the corner of the counter. "I'm going to make a quick call and then maybe I can help you. Since you have to babysit me, you might as well put me to work."

"I don't consider it babysitting."

Morgan wrinkled her nose and picked up the phone. It was a short conversation and one which left her temper climbing. As she slammed the receiver back into the cradle, she whirled to face her mother. "Apparently, Evan's been on the phone."

Diane swiped a flour-covered hand down the front of her apron. "Why's that?"

"He doesn't want to teach me to shoot, and Al down at the shooting range won't do it, either. No doubt Evan's behind that refusal."

Drawing a pan of hot cinnamon rolls from the oven, Diane set them atop a cooling rack. "Now, you don't know that for sure."

Morgan resisted the urge to glare. "Oh, I do, Mom. Trust me. I know Evan Hennessy like I know..." She broke off, clasping her hands in front of her.

"I know." Tugging the quilted mitt from her hand, Diane came forward and took hold of her daughter's hand. "Why don't we sit down and have a cup of coffee? We haven't really taken the time to do that yet, and it looks like it's going to be a slow morning."

"That sounds good."

More than an hour slid by before the first customer walked into the store. The bell over the door clanged, causing Morgan to jump. Diane placed a hand on her shoulder. "It's okay."

Standing, Morgan gripped her mother's arm. "No. It's not okay. Sounds never used to scare me, Mom. Now they do. Sights, sounds, smells—hell, everything scares me. But do you want to know what I'm afraid of the most?" She didn't slow down. "Of something happening to you and Dad. I want you both to leave Skyler."

Diane's eyes narrowed. "I've already told you that's not going to happen."

"Can't you see that it only makes sense?" The customer cleared his throat, and Morgan glared at him.

"How can you even suggest that your father and I leave you alone here?"

"Actually, I was going to suggest the same thing."

Morgan spun around at the sound of Evan's voice, and her hands tingled. The sight of him stirred her, creating ribbons of sensations which danced down her spine. "I didn't hear you come in." Her voice held a breathless quality that made her mother's eyebrows go up.

"I was quiet." He walked over to her. "Diane, Morgan is right."

Diane's chin jutted out at an obstinate angle. "We won't leave our daughter." Her eyes dared Evan to push the matter.

With an irritated noise, the customer turned and practically stomped out of the bakery. As the door clanged shut behind him, Morgan felt the heat of Evan's body as he moved closer to her. "I've already told Mom I can't run."

He nodded. "Then, Diane, I'm afraid I'm going to have to insist you leave. With Canfield setting his sights on Skyler, you're bound to be his first target."

Diane gave him a defiant look, but Morgan saw the touch of helplessness in her eyes. "You can't force us to leave, Evan. Don't even try it."

Morgan watched the battle of wills taking place between her mother, one of the toughest women she knew, and her ex-husband, a former Navy Seal who could give a mule a run for his money.

Finally, Evan shifted his gaze to Morgan's face. "Are you ready to go?"

Her mouth fell open. "That's it? You're going to let it drop?"

"Your mother's mind is made up." He held out his hand.

Morgan avoided it and walked around the table. "I'll call you later, Mom." She got close to Evan's face as she walked by and muttered, "I really don't understand you."

"I like it that way."

Morgan flashed a look over her shoulder and caught the sharp look on Evan's face, and instinct told her Diane and Jack Tanner would leave Skyler that afternoon.

Chapter Ten

Dexter swapped the Lincoln Navigator for a Chevy Tahoe at a small diner in an even smaller town. The driver wouldn't miss it, at least not now. The air conditioner blasted his face as he slid behind the wheel and adjusted the rearview mirror.

Catching a glimpse of his reflection, he grimaced. "Dexter, old boy, you're looking a bit under the weather." He patted his cheeks to restore some color but the same bloodshot eyes stared back at him. "I'd say it's time for a change. After all, I wouldn't want Morgan to recognize me right away. What would be the fun in that?"

He guided the SUV out onto the interstate, careful to keep to the speed limit. He had to limit himself to one cop. Killing another would only draw unwanted attention and God knew Dexter didn't like attention. He chortled at the thought and stomped on the gas.

"Ready or not, dear Morgan, here I come!"

"You haven't told me who Dexter killed," Morgan began once she snapped the seatbelt into place.

Evan slid her a long, contemplative glance and thought about feeding her a lie, but Morgan would read him too easily. "A cop," he responded without any adornment.

He saw her teeth worry her lower lip. "Where was the cop?"

"Just outside Raleigh. He had the misfortune of stopping Canfield for speeding."

Morgan released a breath and knit her fingers together in her lap. "How far outside Raleigh?"

"Not too far," Evan hedged. He saw her frown out of the corner of his eye and began the mental count to ten. He made it to five before Morgan dug for more information.

"How far, Evan?"

"Fifty miles or so. Like I said, not too far."

"Was he heading east or west?"

Evan gripped the steering wheel. He knew Morgan wouldn't withdraw from the conversation until he'd given her all the information he had. "He's coming here, Morgan, but you knew that already."

She directed her gaze out the window. "Yes, I did." She waited a breath of a second before adding, "I talked to Al Wimberly today. He refused to teach me how to shoot."

Evan shifted in his seat. "Yeah, I know. He told me you asked."

Her head turned almost in slow motion. "I guess you did warn me, didn't you?"

Evan knew he would regret his next words. He said them anyway. "I'll teach you."

She adjusted her body toward his. "You're serious?"

He nodded once. "Yeah."

"What made you change your mind?"

He wouldn't tell her Ian. Instead, he lifted one shoulder in a shrug. "You should have the ability to defend yourself if not the opportunity."

Morgan's shoulders relaxed against the seat. "Thank you."

"Don't thank me yet. You've haven't been with me to the firing range."

"What does that mean?"

"I can be a hard teacher."

"I'll keep that in mind."

"I'm being serious, Morgan." *Why was she grinning?*

"I know that, too."

Evan's irritation spiked. "What's going on in that wily brain of yours?"

"You don't think I can do this, do you?"

"Shoot a gun?"

Her lips pursed. "No, play the banjo. Of course, shoot a gun."

He wagged his finger. "Temper, temper." He paused then shrugged. "I'm not sure what to think. You've just always avoided firearms."

Morgan drew a circle on the window with the tip of her finger. "I've changed."

He reached across and touched her knee. "Not all change is bad."

"Did you read that in a Hallmark card?" She grinned.

Evan chuckled. "I don't remember, but it seemed to fit the occasion."

"So can we go now?"

He blinked at her before sliding his gaze back to the road ahead. "Go where?" He played dumb like an expert.

Morgan sighed. "Are you going to be like this all day?"

"Maybe."

"Can we go now?"

He wanted to curse, but instead, he reined in his temper and managed a mild reply. "No, we can't go right now."

"Why not?"

Evan kept his eyes straight ahead. "Because I have a couple of calls to make and I thought you'd like to hang around long enough to say goodbye to your folks."

"I guess I know you too well."

"What does that mean?"

"I suspected you had every intention of sending my parents out of town."

"Well, don't get too smug. I seriously considered sending you."

He felt her eyes on his face and then her soft voice asked. "What made you change your mind?"

Evan gripped the steering wheel. He'd hoped she wouldn't ask that question, but he might have known. Morgan would want the truth, the whole truth and nothing but. He grimaced and the silence while she waited for an answer thickened. "You might not like my answer."

"Were you thinking like a cop?"

The edginess to her voice had him gritting his teeth. "It is the job I do."

She rubbed her eyes with a weary gesture. "You know if I don't stay, you might lose your opportunity to nab Dexter."

"This isn't about the glory of catching him, Morgan."

"I know that." She folded her hands in her lap and Evan waited for her to finish the thought. "You just know if I leave, Dexter will follow me. If I stay, he'll come here."

Evan covered her hands with one of his. "As long as he knows you're here, he won't deviate from his path. That doesn't mean he'll find you when he gets here."

She shot him a look. "What does that mean?"

"I'm not about to let you come face to face with him again."

Morgan seemed to consider the statement and when she drew in a deep breath, Evan knew he wasn't going to like her next words. "I want to come face to face with him again."

The Dodge careened around a corner with a squeal of tires. "Are you out of your mind?" He removed his hand from hers, took his eyes off the road and stared at her face until forced to pay attention to the merging traffic. "Morgan, if you think I'm going to allow you..."

"Hold on a minute," Morgan interrupted, "I don't recall asking your permission."

Evan reigned in his temper with great effort. "Are you trying to push my buttons?"

"No, but is that what I'm doing anyway?"

"I'm trying to help you, Morgan."

She shifted to direct her knees toward him. "I know you are, but you should understand that I have to confront him."

He felt the anger bubbling toward the surface. "No, I don't understand. Correct me if I'm wrong, but haven't you tried to avoid him up until now?"

"Yes, I have, but last night taught me something."

Evan searched through his recall from the previous evening, trying to determine what might have caused her epiphany. He came up blank. "What about last night?"

"I felt the safest I've felt in a long time." She leaned across the console and touched his knee. "And I didn't get a chance to thank you."

His jaw clenched. "I don't want your gratitude, Morgan. I want you to be safe, to let me handle this."

"I will let you handle the law enforcement of this town."

"That's big of you."

Morgan began to stroke his knee through the cotton of his uniform pants. "Evan." She said his name so softly, more of a caress.

Evan felt his defenses crumbling. He never could resist her when she slipped into her persuasive mode. "Do you want to know why I'm so opposed to what you're suggesting?"

"I already know. You're scared Dexter might finish the job he started in Raleigh."

A knife piercing his heart couldn't hurt more than her words did. "I would never allow that."

"Then do you want to know why I'm so determined to see him again?"

His head began to throb. "It's not going to change how I feel about it." He settled his hand atop hers to still the stroking.

Morgan smiled and curled her fingers against his leg. "If I ever want to feel as safe as I felt last night again, I have to confront my demons. Dexter Canfield is my demon."

Evan wouldn't tell her he understood. She'd take it as acceptance. "I don't want you to see him again, Morgan."

"I know, but the next time I face Dexter, I'll be ready for him."

Evan gripped her hand tightly. "We'll be ready for him."

She turned her hand over and moved her fingertips over his palm then the inside of his wrist. "I figured you'd be determined to be there with me."

"Damned straight and if you've got any ideas about trying to stop me, you can just forget..."

"Thanks."

"About it." Evan finished his sentence on a lame note. He eyed her with suspicion. "What are you thanking me for now?"

"For too many reasons to list, but mainly for knowing why I came back to Skyler."

Warmth settled around his heart. He didn't want to fall in love with Morgan all over again. His conscience pricked him at that thought. He couldn't fall in love with someone he'd never stopped loving.

"Evan? You got quiet all of a sudden."

He lifted her hand to his lips and kissed the soft flesh. "I'll take you to the range this evening, and please don't thank me again. This is hard enough without dealing with your gratitude, too."

Morgan sat back against the cushion. "Okay. Fine, but it doesn't change that I am thankful."

"Good. Just keep that to yourself then." He cleared his throat. "Now, we're not going to rush into everything all at once. We'll do this step by step. I'll show you the basics and then you can move at your own pace."

Morgan lifted one eyebrow and Evan saw a twinkle in her green eyes. "Are we still talking about firing a gun?"

He glowered at her. "What else would I be talking about?"

"Finishing what I started this morning."

The truck swerved. "Dammit, Morgan."

She patted his knee in a companionable manner. "Don't worry. I'll make sure I set the pace so you can keep up."

No other woman could turn him inside out like Morgan Tanner. He was in for a long day, and possibly, an even longer night. Not an altogether unpleasant prospect.

Dexter switched off the radio with an angry flick of his wrist. Damned storm was going to beat him to Skyler with the way things were going. He'd stopped once for a flat tire, twice for the radiator overheating and now, the engine light flickered on. He'd stolen a piece of junk. Time to make a trade.

The exit sign for another town stood ahead and Dexter angled the Chevy down the incline. He'd driven like a little old lady for the past hour. His ass hurt, his back ached and his stomach growled. Plainly put, he was damned uncomfortable.

The blinking neon lights of a diner beckoned him and though the outside of the place didn't look too inviting, it was the perfect place to keep a low profile. He killed the engine and sauntered inside. Except for a shapely waitress wiping down the refrigerator, Dexter saw no one else. He allowed himself to relax.

A window unit air conditioner churned in the corner of the diner, providing little, if any, relief from the heat generated by the fryers and griddles. Dexter took position atop a cracked red stool facing the counter and fixed the waitress with a congenial grin. "Evening."

She removed the pen from behind her ear and strolled forward, her steps unhurried. Dexter reckoned his lighter could hurry her up, but he focused on remaining calm. "What'll it be?" She spoke in a soft Southern drawl and the heat from the kitchen added a flush to her cheeks. "You just gonna sit there and stare at me, mister, or are you gonna place an order?"

"Is someone bothering you, Casey?" A big bear of a man poked his head outside a swing door at the end of the counter. He wore a stained white T-shirt and equally stained white pants and on his face, a glower.

Casey patted her hair. "No, Billy. Everything's fine." She tugged a thick pad from the pocket of her apron and fixed her piercing, blue eyes on Dexter's face. "So are you ready, sir?"

Dexter grinned while his insides twisted. That familiar sensation tugged at him and his hand curled against the bulge of his lighter. "Well, let's see here. What would you recommend?" He maintained an affable demeanor.

Casey softened her stance somewhat and leaned in to point out the specials on the plastic menu. "Our meatloaf is always well-liked, and we ain't never had any complaints about our fried chicken, either."

Dexter smacked the menu closed and handed it back across the counter. "Then I guess I'll have the meatloaf."

Casey smiled and turned to place the order.

"Oh, Casey," Dexter called in a non-threatening voice.

The waitress stood on tiptoe to hook the slip of paper to the aluminum wheel overhead before looking over her shoulder. "Yes, sir?"

"You wouldn't happen to know where a guy could grab a good night's sleep, do you?"

The swing door thumped against the wall, and Billy marched out, his moustache practically dancing with irritation. "Buddy, does this look like a travel agency to you?" The man snaked an arm around Casey's waist and tugged her close to his side. "This here's my wife, and she ain't too fond of strangers."

Dexter slid a glance up and down Billy's stout frame. "Apparently, she lost the bet."

Billy's expression darkened, and he released Casey to lunge across the counter, but Dexter reacted quickly. He leapt off the stool and took a swig of his flask.

"That's what's the matter with him! He's drunk!" Casey pointed with her index finger.

As Billy came around the counter, Dexter flicked his lighter in front of his face and spat. The mini-inferno ignited Billy's face, and the man gave a scream to rival any woman.

So much for not drawing attention to himself, Dexter figured. "Hey, Casey, how about tossing me the keys to your car?"

The waitress cried hysterically, rushing to Billy's aid, but Dexter intervened, digging his fingers into her upper arm. "The keys, please, unless you'd like to join your husband here."

"They-they're behind the counter."

"Then you'd best go get them and don't try to call the police, either. Your husband isn't dead, but he very well could be if you pick up that phone."

Casey ran to retrieve her keys and tossed them toward Dexter's chest. "It's the black Honda Accord parked out back. Please, just take it and leave us alone."

Dexter chuckled and dropped the lighter back into his pocket. "I'll take that meatloaf to go."

Casey looked horrified. "Billy's the cook! We own this place. It's just the two of us."

Dexter frowned. He hadn't thought of that. Damn. "Then throw me some things in a bag, whatever you have that's quick." He jutted his chin toward the refrigeration unit. "Some of those pecan pies, a few bags of those potato chips and what else you got?"

Casey stumbled back around behind the counter and quickly filled a brown paper bag with sealed food items. "This is all I've got."

"Throw in a couple cartons of milk and a large soda and I'll be out of your hair."

She did exactly as she was told. Dexter liked that in a woman. He took the bag and backed toward the exit while Billy lay on the floor clawing at his face.

"I'm really sorry I had to do this, ma'am. Really sorry. You were a pretty lady."

Casey stared at him, her mouth rounding to a transfixed circle of horror as Dexter raised the flask to his mouth once more. She barely had time to scream.

Morgan rubbed her hands down her jeans-covered thighs while Evan checked the clip in the semi-automatic handgun. She couldn't take her eyes off the shiny black barrel. The lights from the firing cage gave it an almost evil look.

She heard the snap of the safety catch, and she took a mental step backwards and drew in a deep breath. She'd made this decision. She would stick by it. Evan would not see her fear just as he hadn't seen the tears filing her eyes when she'd said goodbye to her parents a little over an hour ago. She trusted Evan's judgment and though her parents hemmed and hawed and put up a protest, eventually, they'd agreed to depart, but not before wringing a solemn promise from Evan to make sure their daughter didn't get hurt again.

"Morgan?"

She gave a shriek and stumbled backwards. Evan caught her against his chest, preventing the fall. "Are you all right?" He turned her in his arms. "You're pale." He touched his palm to her face. "And perspiring. If you don't want to do this, you don't have to."

Her hands clenched his shirt and she lowered her head to his chest. "No, no. I'm fine. Just a momentary setback." She straightened, pulled herself out of his arms and tugged her T-shirt into place. "I'm ready."

Evan tucked the gun into the waistband of his jeans. "Okay, let's start with the basics. This is a .22 caliber semi-automatic. Each time you pull the trigger, it fires one bullet."

Morgan's hands began to sweat. "You mean as opposed to two or three?"

Evan kept a straight face. Morgan admired him for that. "Only automatic weapons fire more than one bullet at a time."

She ran her hands down her jeans again. "Okay. Sorry. Just a little levity."

He touched her arm. "Are you sure you want to do this?"

She bobbed her head and swallowed hard. "Just keep going."

"Okay. Fine." As Evan began to relay the intricacies of the gun and an in-depth description of its capabilities, Morgan listened with one ear, but she watched the gun with both eyes.

"Next, we're going to talk about your stance."

Morgan blinked at him. "My stance?"

"You have to assume a certain posture to maintain good balance and to hit the target." He came to stand behind her and placed his hands on her hips.

"Is this really part of the lesson?"

He laughed. "It really is. The rest of your lesson comes later."

Morgan's blood heated. "I'll hold you to that."

He slid his hands down the front of her body to rest his palms against her thighs. "You want to assume what's called a boxer's stance. Keep your pelvis at a forty-five degree angle in relation to your target. You'll maintain proper weight distribution and..." His hands slipped up to rest at her waist. "And..." He stopped talking again.

Morgan leaned back against him. "Yes?"

His fingers tugged her T-shirt free of her jeans. "And I didn't realize this would be so hard."

"Are you talking about teaching me how to shoot?"

He spun her around. "Not at all." He kissed her almost violently, pressing her against him so tightly the butt of the pistol jabbed against her abdomen. Morgan didn't complain. She wrapped her arms around his neck and threw herself into the sensations.

Evan backed her toward the wall, moving so fast they stumbled over the concrete floor. Hands flew across clothing, tearing at the fibers until fingertips could touch skin. When Evan's palms first touched the scars on Morgan's side, she tensed, but he maintained a soft caress, gentle, and she began to relax, melting once more.

She hooked one leg around his calf and dragged him closer, knotting her hands in the silky strands of his hair. His unshaven jaw scratched her cheek and the buttons of his shirt jabbed her breasts, but she held on, tight enough to feel alive.

Evan kissed her without restraint, his lips savaging hers. Tongue met tongue, dancing, stroking until Morgan's blood flowed through her veins like a sluggish river.

"We've got to stop this," Evan whispered while Morgan tugged his shirt free of his jeans.

"Yeah, I know," she responded on a gasp.

He shoved the hem of her T-shirt up to her collarbone and found her nipple through the lacy cup of her bra. His fingers tantalized her before he drew the peak into his mouth.

Morgan arched her spine against the brick and held his head in place. Their breaths stabbed the air, coming in pants and whispers. Evan raked the zipper of her jeans down and palmed her womanhood. She pushed against his hand, every nerve in her body humming.

141

Without warning, the overhead lights fizzled, crackled and died out. Evan whipped his body around, pressing his back against Morgan's chest. She felt his muscles tensing, and her own heart hammered within her chest.

"Never can figure out these damned lights."

Morgan heard a voice she didn't recognize, and a scream bubbled up in her throat. She heard Evan's breath escape his lungs in a long, low curse.

"Dammit, Ian!"

Hysteria made Morgan clamp her hand over her mouth, and while she remained frozen in position, Evan righted her clothes.

"Turn the damned lights back on!" Evan shouted over his shoulder.

"I'm trying to!" An older voice responded in a peevish tone. "I don't know why they have to make these things so difficult."

Evan smacked the wall above Morgan's head. "It's an up-switch. What's so difficult?"

The lights snapped on and the fluorescence flooded the firing pen. Evan cupped Morgan's cheek. "Are you all right?"

She barely had time to nod before a wizened old man wearing overalls and a chambray work shirt ambled into view. With a baseball cap turned backwards and a sideways grin, he reminded Morgan of Otis from the Andy Griffith Show. Morgan kept her hand over her mouth while Evan pivoted to face their visitor. She finally began to relax. She remembered Ian, though she hadn't seen him since her return to Skyler. He'd always had the worst timing even when she'd known him years ago. Just another one of those things that didn't change.

"What in the hell are you doing out here? You scared the hell out of Morgan."

Ian waggled a finger in Evan's direction. "Don't take that tone with me. I thought you were out here by yourself."

Evan breathed out a sigh and indicated Morgan with a sweep of his hand. "Morgan, I'm sure you remember Ian."

Ian scraped his hat off his head. "Of course she remembers me. It's good to see you, lady."

Morgan managed a wobbly smile though her knees felt as if they wouldn't hold her aloft for much longer.

Ian scratched his head and swiveled a glance between Morgan and Evan. "Did I interrupt something?"

Morgan lowered her head and let Evan supply the answer. He didn't.

"What did you need?"

Morgan looked up in time to see Ian grin slyly. "Apparently, I did. Well, never you mind what I wanted now. I reckon it can wait." He clamped the battered baseball cap back onto his head and began a backwards shuffle toward the heavy, metal door leading outside. "It was good to see you again, Morgan."

Evan cursed again and held up one finger. "Hold on a second, Morgan. I need to find out what he's doing here."

Evan followed Ian at a trot. "Wait a minute! You don't come looking for me unless you got something important to tell me. Now, what's going on?"

Ian stopped walking and shoved his hands into the pockets of his denim overalls. "It ain't nothin'. I'm telling you. It can wait. Honestly, boy, I didn't mean to interrupt."

Evan mentally counted to ten. "Well, since I've already come after you and," he lowered his voice, "nothing is going to happen now, you might as well appease my curiosity."

Ian chortled and smacked Evan on the shoulder. "Damn, but you move fast."

Evan didn't want to discuss what almost happened between him and Morgan. "So what's the news?"

Ian peeled the cap from his head once more and dusted it against his leg. "Me and Mae are getting married."

"Mae Haggerty?"

Ian squared his shoulders as if preparing for a fight. "We are and I don't want to hear it."

Evan raised one eyebrow. "Hear what?"

"Whatever smart-assed comment you have in mind."

Evan grinned. "Congratulations, Ian."

The old man turned beet red and returned the cap to its former position. "Now, if you'll hurry up, we can make it a double wedding."

Evan heard the swift intake of breath behind him.

"Damn," Ian muttered. "I always did have rotten timing." He didn't look at Morgan before he made his getaway, leaving Evan to deal with the fallout.

"You know Ian. He always thinks before he speaks." Evan tried to brush off the conversation, but as he walked toward Morgan, she held up one hand.

"We should go. I didn't even realize what time it was." She left him standing as she walked toward the Dodge.

Evan crammed his hands into the pockets of his jeans and strode after her, cursing Ian with each step.

Chapter Eleven

Dexter sauntered toward the bathroom attached to the small, brick building housing the gas station. With grocery bag in hand, he slipped into the dimly lit room. He didn't pay much attention to the litter on the floor or the suggestive markings on the wall.

He'd barely adjusted the wig on his head when someone thumped on the door. "I'll be out in a few minutes," he called in response, never increasing his pace. He had to make sure he looked just right when he saw Morgan again. And the last thing he wanted was instant recognition.

"Hey, buddy, you coming out today?" came an irate voice from the other side of the flimsy door.

Dexter shot an angry glare over his shoulder. "Didn't I just say a few minutes?"

A fist banged again. "Some of us have to go."

"You think I'm in here because I like the décor?"

The man on the other side made a rude comment then silence descended. Dexter took a deep breath to refocus his attention on the matter at hand and fixed his eyes on the cracked glass in front of him.

He tapped his new, shaggy, brown hair and grinned. "Not too bad, Canfield, even if I do say so myself. Now, where did I put those contacts?"

Morgan sat on the edge of the guest bed, kicking her feet against the dust flap. As night fell, she could think of a million and one things she wanted to do now, all of which required the presence of her ex-husband.

As if reading her mind, Evan came up the stairs and approached the open doorway. He leaned one shoulder against the doorframe and peeked into the room. "You okay?"

She straightened and gave him a semi-believable nod.

He cleared his throat. "Well, okay. I'm sure you're tired. I'll just leave you alone, let you get some rest." He turned to leave and Morgan knew she should let him go. She didn't want to face a morning filled with regrets. She didn't need yet one more worry in her life.

She heard Evan's booted feet hit the top step and she called his name. She didn't stop to think as she rushed after him. He paused, one hand on the banister, hazel eyes fixed on her face. "Could you, do you think you could stay with me for a little while?"

Without question, Evan backtracked toward her. "I thought you might be feeling nervous. Do you want me to get you a glass of brandy or something to help calm you down?" He touched her arm as he brushed past her into the bedroom. "Even better, why don't I draw you a bath? It seemed to help before and..." The bedroom door clicked shut, effectively silencing the remainder of his speech. His gaze flew from her hand, which still held the doorknob, to her face.

"I'm not nervous, Evan, at least not about what you think." Her hand fell to her side.

Evan took a step toward the bed. "Morgan, maybe you should think about what you're doing."

"You don't think I have thought about it?" She flicked her hair over her shoulders and watched Evan's gaze climb up her body. "It's all I can think about since I came back to Skyler. Maybe this is the reason I came back. I knew, if there was one person who could take my mind off Raleigh, it was you. That might be wrong and I'm sorry. I may be using you, Evan." She stopped speaking to give him a chance to digest her words. When he remained silent, she continued in a low, husky voice wrapped in seduction. "Would you rather I go to bed alone?"

One long stride brought him face to face with her and one second later, he'd dragged her into his arms.

And Morgan had her answer.

The tie choked him. He'd always hated the damnable things. Dexter tried not to tug at the expensive silk as he walked into the drab interior of the gas station. He strolled to the back cooler, extracted an icy soda and then made his way to the counter with a charming smile on his face.

But the cashier paid him no attention. She'd focused her eyes on the Chevy Tahoe parked directly in front of the plate glass window. She shifted her stance when Dexter put his purchase down on the counter in front of him.

Dexter tossed a butane filler next to the soda and added a pack of chewing gum and a chocolate bar. "How much do I owe you?"

The girl darted a look out the window and Dexter saw her eyes flick to the front of the Honda. He angled a look over his shoulder and took notice of the garish vanity plate on the front bumper. Vivid red with gold wings circling a Harley-Davidson motorcycle, the plate bore the names of Billy and Casey in white script. Dexter cursed below his breath. He hated to make a mistake, but this was a definite mistake.

He stuck his hand into the pocket of his pants. "I asked the price, ma'am." He forced himself to remain calm. Apparently, an APB had been issued for the Honda and no doubt, the local police had made mention of the license plate. Probably the only link the yokels had to the former owners of the burned-down diner.

The cashier rang up his purchases with speed born of fear and Dexter watched her with his lip curling. Stupid bitch. She probably wanted him to hustle along so she could call the police and claim whatever reward had been posted, if indeed, one had been. He suspected if the owners' bodies had been discovered, there would be.

"That will be six dollars and twenty-nine cents, sir." The cashier's voice squeaked and her hand shook when she held it out for the money.

Dexter caught a glimpse of the small butterfly tattoo gracing her wrist. "Nice tattoo."

The girl withdrew her hand in an instant. "Thank you." She kept an eye out toward the door and Dexter wondered if she'd somehow already managed to call the police while he'd been distracted at the cooler. He held out a ten-dollar bill and kept a congenial smile pasted on his face until the young woman took hold.

"I can't help but notice that you're paying a lot of attention to my vehicle."

The cashier punched the wrong button on the register and frantically tried to find the right one. "Um, no, sir. I haven't, that is, I like cars. I like to look at different ones."

Dexter's good humor returned at the lame excuse. "Really? Your interest wouldn't have anything to do with that plate on the front, would it?"

The register drawer shot open and the girl dug into the stack of one-dollar bills. "I, um, no, I, don't really, that is, I haven't really noticed it at all." She made a show out of looking out the window. "Oh, that license plate." She gave a nervous giggle and crammed his change back into his hand. "I hadn't noticed it."

Dexter curled his fingers over the money. "Really? Hmmm. That's funny because I specifically saw you looking at it." The cashier began to bag up the merchandise while he leaned one hip against the counter and watched her jerky movements. "Is there some reason why you're so agitated, ma'am?"

He saw her tongue flick out to moisten her lips. "No, of course not. Have a good day, sir." She stressed the words, as if by the sheer force of her will, she could coerce him to leave.

Dexter chuckled and withdrew the car keys from the front pocket of his pants. He made a show out of jingling the ring. "You do the same." He turned to walk toward the door and then stopped. "You know," he tossed a look over his shoulder, "you should really think about paying more attention to your customers and less attention to their automobiles. Minding your own business can certainly make your life a lot easier."

The cashier bobbed her head in rapid agreement. "Yes, sir. Absolutely, sir. You're right."

He gave her a two-fingered salute and edged open the glass door. From the corner of his eye, he saw the young woman stumble toward the back counter. Grinning, he strolled toward the Honda, taking his sweet time. Instincts told him the exact moment when the cashier reached for the telephone.

His fingers curled around the lighter in his pocket, and he clicked his tongue against the roof of his mouth. Some people obviously couldn't take advice.

He spun on his heel and meandered back into the small convenience store. The cashier dropped the receiver so fast, she missed the cradle altogether. "Did you forget something, sir?" Her fingers curled around the edge of the counter, and Dexter heard every breath she took. Her chest rose and fell in rapid succession, and he heard the hope in her voice, but he didn't answer her shaky question. Instead, he held the lighter up for her inspection and when her eyes widened, a surge of adrenaline pumped through him. "You know, I was going to let you live."

The moonlight played over her body as Morgan freed herself from her clothing. With each piece she removed, she gave herself permission to be a woman again. She watched Evan's eyes darken with desire and knew he didn't see the scars. He saw her and maybe images of the past, but she wouldn't complain.

He stretched out across the quilt, his head propped in his hand. She'd asked for this, had wanted to give herself the chance to shake free of the events in Raleigh. She did an impromptu pirouette when only her lacy panties remained. Though Evan drew in a deep breath, she still had a moment's hesitation, a slight dent in her self-confidence. She stopped turning and stepped into the shadows, out of the glow of the moon.

"Don't," Evan commanded in a voice she recognized from times past. Those times, he'd wanted her and now, as he pushed himself off the mattress and walked toward her, she saw that same look again. He couldn't hide his body's reaction to hers and she enjoyed every inch of that knowledge.

"You want me," she whispered when he came within arm's reach of her.

He brushed his knuckles over her cheek. "I thought we'd been over that."

She thrust her chin back and in an almost challenging voice, reminded him. "I'm scarred."

He took hold of her hand and placed it over his heart. "And you're beautiful."

She looked into the hazel depths of his eyes and for a brief second, she could almost believe he didn't see the damage the fire had caused. And then it didn't matter. He reached for her again, meshing her body with his and the scars faded to the back of her mind, replaced by powerful, almost savage memories of years gone by, nights of shared passion and intimacy she'd missed for years.

Evan nuzzled her neck and heat shot through to her core. "God, I've missed you," he muttered.

She reached for his hands and placed them over her breasts. "I need you to touch me."

He lifted his head and his eyes sparked. "With pleasure." He palmed the firm globes of flesh and began a delicious assault.

Morgan kept her eyes on his face, watching for any sign of revulsion.

Suddenly, Evan dropped his hands. "Stop." The harsh word made her blink at him.

"Stop what? I don't understand."

"Don't you?" Evan grabbed hold of her shoulders and gave her a slight shake. "You are waiting for the axe to fall, for that moment when I'll look away from you because I can't stand to see the scars." At her indrawn breath, he plowed on. "If you're looking for honesty, I'll give it to you. No, I can't stand to see the scars but not for the reason you think."

She licked her lips and hung on every word. "Then why?"

"Because I know what you endured to get those scars. You lived through hell, Morgan, but it doesn't change the beautiful, passionate, vibrant woman I know you to be." He captured handfuls of her hair. "Let me show you what you've forgotten."

She tipped her head back and met his challenging stare. "Yes."

He didn't say another word.

The night exploded with fierce touches, the whispered words of renewed passion and soft sounds of pleasure.

Evan guided her toward the bed and lowered her to the mattress, fanning her hair out around her face. She looked up into his ruggedly handsome face and for a brief moment, time faded, and they were man and wife again.

Allowing herself the luxury of relearning the beauty of his body, she slid her hands over each corded muscle. Her palm covered his heart, and his hand captured hers. They froze together, locked in their gazes while the beats resonated through their joined hands.

"That's what you do to me, Morgan."

She closed her eyes on a sigh and for that moment, if only for that moment, chose to believe him. His lips brushed her neck, her clavicle, before he swept kisses down over her breasts. He feasted on her nipples, wringing cries of both torment and pleasure from her lips.

Then he traveled even lower, moving over the smooth terrain of her flat abdomen before pausing over the warmth nestled between her thighs. She held her breath while his breath caressed her intimately.

His fingers drew circles over her thighs. "You're so soft."

Instinctively, she parted her legs and Evan took advantage of the opening. He slid one hand lower and the pads of his fingers smoothed the crease he found there.

Morgan's heart began a staccato rhythm. She remembered well the mastery of Evan's hands and mouth on her body. He knew exactly where to touch her, how to touch her and he didn't stop until she cried out from sheer exhaustion.

Her legs moved restlessly atop the quilt and Evan dipped his head again. With his mouth, he destroyed her defenses and all inhibitions disintegrated. She welcomed each stroke of his tongue and fisted her hands in his hair to hold him in place.

When the release broke through her barriers, Evan joined her at the top of the bed, his lips everywhere, creating glistening patches of moisture over her skin. She moved against him with reckless abandon, placing his hands where she wanted them most, unmindful of the grim reminders of the past several weeks.

She dragged his lips to hers and supped at his mouth. "Take me, Evan," she implored on a ragged breath. "I need to feel you inside me."

He didn't protest. He simply followed her instructions, rising over her. He captured her gaze and her heart, his eyes never leaving her face. She knew what he wanted. Their eyes would remain connected as long as their bodies. They would reach climax together, their breaths uniting in the darkness of the room.

Evan slid his hands behind her thighs and shifted her legs. His hips nudged her thighs wider and Morgan held her breath in anticipation, waiting for that first moment of perfection.

The tip of his sex brushed hers and she grasped his forearms. Waiting. Impatient. He glided into her slowly, stretching the walls of her feminine core. Morgan's breath released on a sigh of heady contentment.

Hazel eyes held her gaze securely as Evan began to move, to intensify the pressure building within the union. "You still feel perfect," he whispered.

Tears pricked at the backs of her eyes. "So do you." She raised her legs and locked them around his hips. "Now, stop treating me like a fragile piece of china."

Evan's lips curled upwards into a grin and grabbing hold of her hips, he began to thrust into her, increasing the speed. As he stroked that certain spot within her sex, Morgan felt the scream bubbling in the back of her throat.

Her muscles tensed, coiled and then released, unfurling as seismic waves rolled over her. She cried out his name, dug her nails into his shoulders, and arched her back off the mattress.

Evan stiffened and Morgan watched the intensity of the release seize him. He held himself aloft with his hands next to her head until his arms gave way. Morgan welcomed both the weight and the shelter of his body. She buried her face in his shoulder and wrapped her arms around his back, holding him close.

She didn't want to talk and Evan seemed to sense it. He finally shifted and took her with him, drawing her into the nest of his arms. Her head found his chest and her hands curled over his heart.

For the first time in a very long time, as sleep beckoned her, she didn't fear the darkness.

He arrived in Hooterville fifteen minutes before midnight. Perfect time to slip in unnoticed. He parked the Honda Accord in the parking lot of a small motel and stepped out into the brisk night air. He welcomed the chill and, lighting a cigarette, made his way to the front office, jingling the keys in his pocket.

The desk clerk looked bored but harmless. Dexter gave the young man a congenial smile. "How much for a room?"

"Forty dollars without cable, forty-five with."

Dexter slid a fifty across the cracked countertop. "I'd like cable, please."

The post-adolescent swiped the cash and plunked a plastic key ring with one key onto the counter next to Dexter's hand. "Check out's at eleven. No pets."

Dexter itched to shake the boy up some, but figured he was better off not making waves. At least for now. Plenty of time to do that. He scooped up the key and turned away, pausing to ask, "By the way, I just passed a bakery on the way into town tonight. What time does that open in the morning?"

The clerk looked up and scratched his head. "Usually about five, but it's closed now."

"Oh, really?" Dexter knew he sounded appropriately disappointed.

"Yeah. Owners are out of town."

"Well, just my luck." Striving for affability, Dexter pushed open the glass door. The bell overhead jangled. "Goodnight then."

"Night. Oh, and welcome to Skyler."

Dexter wanted to add "sir", but he figured the youth wouldn't respond to that type of correction. He fingered the lighter in his pocket but squelched the urge.

"Focus, Dexter. Focus. You're not here for him. You're here for one woman and one woman only." He walked back to the car and smacked the hood.

"Welcome to Skyler, indeed."

Chapter Twelve

Evan cracked open one eye and found the pillow next to his empty. His other eye opened. "Morgan?" He pushed himself to a sitting position and swung his legs over the side of the bed, taking time to allow his head to clear from deep sleep. And it had been a damned good night's sleep. He couldn't remember the last one he had like that.

He stood and stretched, catching the scent of coffee in the air. He inhaled with an appreciative grin and sauntered to the bedroom door. Morgan had closed it to allow him to sleep. Little things like that made him remember all too well the better portions of their marriage.

He scratched his stomach and dropped one hand to the doorknob just as Morgan pushed against the door. He stepped back quickly, moving out of her way as she entered carrying two mugs of steaming coffee. He watched her carry them both to the table next to his side of the bed.

"I hope you still like yours black." Morgan had already showered and Evan inhaled the fragrance of her shampoo. She smelled fresh and touchable.

He didn't waste time on good morning pleasantries. Instead, he strode toward her. She turned and he saw the momentary surprise on her face as he hauled her into his arms.

Then she yielded against his naked chest, raising her chin to give him full access to her lips.

Evan snagged hold of her hips and held her in place, rocking the lower half of his body against hers. When he raised his head, he gave her a wink and whispered, "Now that's what I call a good morning." Red colored her cheeks and he grinned. "And I do still take my coffee black."

"Creature of habit," Morgan murmured, lifting her own mug of coffee. She settled herself down on the edge of the bed and tucked one stray lock of soft blonde hair behind her ear. She curled her lips around the rim of the mug and blew gently.

Holy hell. Evan turned around before Morgan saw the raging erection. She still cooled her coffee the same way. And he still reacted the same way.

"You're not very talkative this morning." Morgan patted the mattress beside her. "Don't you want to sit and have some coffee with me?"

He kept his back to her while thinking of anything to cool his rabid hormones. "Um. Yeah. Just a minute, though. Need to, um." He pointed toward the bathroom.

Morgan smiled over her shoulder. "Oh."

He wondered if she watched his rump as he walked away. Not that he minded, but the thought only served to make the situation harder. Pun intended.

Morgan smiled to herself once Evan disappeared. Apparently, he'd expected regrets and recriminations instead of the serenity he saw. She took a sip of the coffee and waited patiently for him to return. When he finally reappeared, damp tendrils of hair curled around his face and he wore a towel low on his hips.

Evan cleared his throat. "I'm going to grab a pair of jeans first."

She looked at him over the rim of her mug. "Are you nervous?"

He stopped walking. "Nervous? What are you talking about?"

"You're acting strange."

He rescued last night's jeans and stuffed his feet into the leg holes one at a time. He didn't respond to her comment until he tugged the denim up over his hips. "You knew what I was expecting, Morgan." He eyed her over his shoulder.

She gave him a serene smile. "Regrets."

He zipped the jeans. "Damned right."

"And you're upset that I'm not regretting last night."

"Yes." He shook his head. "No. I'm not upset about it. I'm confused."

She thumped the mattress next to her thigh. "It's about time I was able to confuse you. Now, sit down and drink your coffee."

He walked toward the bed. "What's the rush?"

"I want to go to the range again." She paused and flashed him an impish smile. "But this time, I actually want to shoot the gun."

Dexter stepped out into the morning sunshine, stretching his arms high over his head. Damn, it felt good to be alive. He lit up a cigarette and leaned one shoulder against the doorframe to the hotel room.

A couple of portly housekeepers rolled their carts by on the second story concrete and murmured good morning. Dexter responded with two fingers to his temple.

"He looks familiar."

The words brought his hand up short. Suspended in air halfway to his mouth, the cigarette dangled from his fingertips. He looked familiar? Dexter brought his free hand to his head and realized he'd forgotten the damned wig.

Muttering curses, he slammed back inside the darkened room. What was wrong with him? He didn't make mistakes. Mistakes were for incompetent people. He could never be considered incompetent.

He'd earned a law degree and practiced law at one of the most prestigious law firms in North Carolina, all while eluding the police for the past three years. He'd littered the entire Tarheel state with dead bodies and still hadn't been discovered. Hell, once, he'd even ventured into South Carolina and took out a couple visiting from Florida just to watch them burn.

He clamped the wig on top of his crew cut and secured it in place. No, he didn't make mistakes, at least not regularly. He'd have to make sure this didn't happen again. But first, he had to make sure the housekeeper's memory didn't kick in and remind her where she'd seen him. Then, he'd make sure her friend didn't know anything.

The morning was off to a good start.

Morgan closed one eye and squeezed the trigger of the .22 caliber pistol. The report of the bullet sounded loud to her ears even though she wore earmuffs. She winced and lowered the weapon. "Did I hit it?" She pointed to the target.

"Depends," Evan drawled. "Did you intend to hit the copyright notice?"

She tore off the goggles, pushed the muffs back and glared at him. "That's not funny."

Evan reeled the target in. "I'm not laughing."

As the bull's-eye came into view, Morgan saw she had hit the tiny row of letters at the bottom of the printed sheet. Damn. She hunched her shoulders. "Okay. Send it back out."

Evan came up behind her and settled his hands on her shoulders. "Maybe we should take a break. You've been at this for over an hour."

She shook her head mutinously. "I'm not giving up until I put a bullet in the center of that target."

Evan's cheeks puffed out as he exhaled. "I should have packed a lunch."

"Evan!" She whirled on him. "I need your support not your grumbles."

He lifted his shoulders in a defensive shrug. "Sorry. Have you forgotten we skipped breakfast?"

Her skin tingled. How could she have forgotten that? After taking two sips of his coffee, Evan decided he wanted something a bit different to start off his day. He'd pushed her back against the mattress and took her with a ferocity Morgan matched. She lowered her eyes from his. "So go grab a sandwich. I'm going to stay here and practice."

"I'm not leaving you alone here."

"I think I'm fairly safe."

"I'm not worried about you as much as I am any low-flying birds."

She smacked his shoulder so hard her palm stung. "Go away."

Evan chuckled and grabbed her around the waist, easily securing the pistol in his right hand. "Come on. Aren't you getting hungry?"

Her stomach rumbled in response and she grinned up into his mischievous, hazel eyes. She missed these times. The freedom, the sense of unity, had been missing from her life for over five years now.

"Hey, are you still with me?" Evan caught hold of her chin.

She blinked the moisture away from her eyes before he could see the sheen. "Of course I'm with you. Where else would I be?"

"Knock-knock," Deputy Chadwick announced his arrival before he stuck his head into the firing pen. "Hey, Sheriff. Ian said I might find you here."

Evan's brows lowered. "Ian knows too much about my life."

The deputy removed his hat and his hair stood on end. "Umm, could I talk with you for a minute?"

Morgan picked up on the deputy's discomfort. "What's wrong?"

Chadwick jerked his head toward Morgan, red creeping up his face. "I don't think, that is, this is something you might want to tell her yourself."

Evan steered Morgan back toward the Plexiglas window. "Why don't you wait here? I'll be right back."

"I'd rather you just go ahead and tell me while you're here, Deputy Chadwick."

The deputy shifted from foot to foot, clearly caught in the line of fire. "Well, ma'am—"

"I'll tell you as soon as I know what's going on," Evan interjected.

"You'll tell me the watered-down version," she objected. "I want the unedited version."

"You'll know soon enough." He started to walk away, but Morgan snagged hold of the sleeve of his T-shirt.

"I want to know now." She stared into his hard-eyed gaze and though his lips tightened with disapproval, she didn't back down. "I mean it, Evan."

He glared at her.

She glared back.

He finally relented with a grunt. "Fine." He waved a hand toward the fidgeting deputy. "You might as well say what you have to say."

The young man's discomfort grew. "Well, Sheriff, I, uh, that is, I don't really know if this is something I should be saying in front of Mrs. Hennessy."

Evan scrubbed the back of his neck. "Just say it."

Chadwick looked down at the ground. "Just up the road a ways, a diner was set ablaze. Police found two bodies inside. Haven't been able to identify them yet." He tugged at his tie before continuing. "Then, Bart's gas station was set on fire late last night. Andrea was caught inside." He raised his head to give Morgan an apologetic look. "Andrea's just a young girl, not more than twenty. She's been working there part-time to put herself through college. Hospital said she might make it." The deputy clamped his hat back on his head. "Anyways, Sheriff, I thought you'd want to know."

"Thanks," Evan responded.

Morgan felt the blood run cold in her veins. "So last night, Dexter Canfield was just outside of town. Odds are good he's here now."

Evan dismissed the deputy with a short jerk of his head before turning his attention back to Morgan. "Do you want to go home? If you feel safer there, I'll take you."

She settled the earmuffs back into place.

"Morgan?" He tapped her shoulder.

"I want to shoot." Even she heard the conviction in her own voice. She wanted to know, before she saw Dexter again, that she could put a bullet between his eyes if she had to.

And unless a miracle occurred, she would face him again, but this time, she wouldn't be a victim.

Evan double-checked the Tanners' property, reassuring himself that the locks were firmly in place. He walked around the house, his hand on the butt of his .9mm. Nothing seemed out of place and yet, the next-door neighbor's frantic phone message had prompted him to pay a visit. Even now, he saw the older lady peeking out through a fold in the heavy drapes obscuring her front bay windows. He lifted a hand to acknowledge her presence and the curtain dropped back into place.

He knelt down at the back steps and checked the ground for fresh footprints, but saw nothing. Whatever Mrs. Baker had seen, she hadn't seen a potential intruder here. He began to push himself to his feet, a little more relaxed.

His cell phone trilled and he responded to the summons by barking his last name.

"Good afternoon, Sheriff Hennessy."

Evan stilled. "Who is this?" His heart sped up.

"You mean you honestly don't know?"

The creepy voice sent a cold chill down Evan's spine. "Canfield."

Dexter Canfield chuckled, but it was more of an eerie, morose sound. "So you do recognize my voice."

"No, but I know you."

"Have we met?"

Evan walked toward his car. "No, but we will soon enough."

Canfield gave another abrupt laugh. "You have something I want."

Evan's temples began to throb. "Morgan isn't a something. She's a someone."

"Semantics." Canfield cackled. "We can do this one of two ways. I can take it easy on this town."

"You mean like you did with the gas station attendant?"

Canfield clicked his tongue in reproof. "You're interrupting me and the gas station shouldn't concern you as much as your ex-wife should." He fell silent and Evan felt the sweat popping out on the back of his neck. "Now, this time, don't interrupt. I hate to repeat myself. As I was saying, I can take it easy on this town and leave only with the woman I came for or I can wreak havoc and leave it with what I came for. The choice is yours."

Evan resisted the urge to hurl the cell phone across the Tanners' back yard. "What makes you so sure you'll be able to leave at all?"

"Have the police caught me yet, Hennessy?"

"That was them. You haven't dealt with me before."

"So you're saying I should be worried about a small-town sheriff, then?"

Evan's fingers tightened around the butt of his gun. "If I were you, I'd be very worried."

"Then consider me worried." Evan heard the smirk in the killer's voice. "In the meantime, I think you're going to have your hands full convincing the lovely Mrs. Hennessy to stay inside."

Evan slammed the door of the truck and turned the key in the ignition. "I've met guys like you before, Canfield, and they all want the same thing."

"What's that?" Canfield sounded bored.

"Notoriety. I'll give you what you want." Evan stomped the accelerator. "The death of a noted serial killer will make top headlines on every newspaper across the country."

Canfield began to laugh again. "You sound very sure of yourself, Sheriff, and I'd love to continue this conversation. But I see someone I really must talk to. That's a beautiful yellow blouse Morgan is wearing today, isn't it?"

The dial tone resounded in Evan's ear and he let loose with a stream of invectives. He punched in his home number but the voice mail answered. "Dammit! Answer the damned phone!" he shouted to the interior of the car.

He racked his brain, trying to remember what color blouse Morgan wore. Had she changed clothes? He swore she was wearing a pink knit top this morning. He dialed the station and got Chadwick on the phone. "Canfield's in town. He just called me. Said he saw Morgan. She was supposed to stay inside. I left her at my house long enough to drive to the Tanners. I need you to find her."

"I'm on it."

Evan heard Chadwick's boots hit the floor followed by the slam of the office door. Then the deputy disconnected him.

Morgan stood at the window just inside the door of Evan's house, watching as the town's citizens passed by. They smiled and waved, unaware of the monster who waited just beyond the town's limits.

Wrapping her arms around herself, she rested her head against the pane, forcing herself to relax, to think about something other than the danger that lay ahead.

Evan. He seemed to be the sole focus of her thoughts these days. Being with him. Seeing him. Touching him. In his arms, she felt whole again.

The wind carried a Frisbee high in the air, and the chatter of excited children drew Morgan's gaze to the yard across the street. Two, exuberant boys raced down the sidewalk, each trying to reach the flying disc first. She heard the good-natured tussle, and she smiled.

She'd come home. At least for now. There was no way to predict what would happen once Dexter descended upon Skyler, but she had to believe that he wouldn't win this time.

Chapter Thirteen

The Dodge's engine screamed as Evan demanded more speed. The pickup roared into the center of town and his eyes scanned the sidewalks, searching for any sign of Morgan. She couldn't have left the house, could she? Not when he'd told her to stay inside. No, she wouldn't want to risk coming face to face with Dexter again.

But how did the maniac know about the blouse? Evan didn't want to think about it. Instincts on high alert, he lifted his foot off the accelerator, slowing down to a moderate pace. There were too many people milling around to risk the speed.

He saw Ian chatting with a couple of the old-timers who spent the better part of their days sitting on the steps of the town hall. Mrs. Eldridge pushed her great-granddaughter's baby carriage toward Elm Street, and Ed Barkley followed her in the hopes of getting up the courage to ask her out.

But who he didn't see was Morgan. Hope made his heart beat quicker. Maybe Dexter had been bluffing. Could the blouse have just been a lucky guess? Did he know yellow was Morgan's favorite color?

Sweat ran down the back of Evan's neck. Yeah, maybe that was it. Just a coincidence.

The knock on the door surprised her. Uncertainty dogged her steps as she walked to answer the summons. The peephole afforded her little information other than a dark-haired man with wire-rimmed glasses. "Yes?"

"Mrs. Elridge?"

Her shoulders sagged with relief. The voice on the other end of the door held a heavy Southern accent. "I'm sorry. You have the wrong house."

The man outside the door tipped his baseball cap in a gentlemanly fashion. "My apologies, ma'am. Would you happen to know where she lives? Her son's a friend of mine, and I wanted to just stop in and say hello."

A chill coursed through her veins. Maybe Evan's dire warnings had finally taken root. Or perhaps she'd simply lost her trust in mankind. "I'm sorry. I don't."

"Very well then. I'm sorry to bother you."

He pivoted and started down the steps. And the sound of a chuckle caused her heart to clench. She could have sworn she'd heard that laugh before. Goosebumps littered her arms.

Hadn't she?

Evan brought the truck to a screeching halt outside his house and throwing the gearshift into park, he leaped out onto the concrete. After fumbling with his keys for several seconds, he barreled inside with his heart racing like a runaway locomotive.

"Morgan! Morgan, are you here?" Before he could dash up the stairs, she came out of the kitchen.

"I'm right here."

Relief pouring through him, he ran toward her, capturing her in his arms. He slammed her against his chest and held on tight. "Thank God." He breathed in the scent of her hair, an intoxicating blend of honeysuckle and strawberries. "You're all right."

"What's wrong with you?"

He gave himself one more luxurious minute holding her before he pushed her away. "Dammit! Why can't you stay put?" One hand fisted in the hem of her gaily-colored blouse. Yellow. The knowledge was like a sucker punch to his gut.

Morgan stared up at him for a brief second before she peeled his fingers away from her top. "Why are you acting like this? Something's happened, hasn't it?"

His teeth snapped, and every nerve in his body tensed. "What's going on is that you can't follow orders."

"Could you be more specific?"

"You left the house today." His temper soared. "Jesus, Morgan! I'm trying to save your life!"

"I never left the house." Her voice dropped a notch.

He grabbed hold of her shoulders and gave her a slight shake. "You didn't answer my phone or your cell. Tell me you're not lying to me."

"I'm not lying to you, Evan. I wouldn't leave the house with Dexter out there somewhere. God only knows how close he is." She shivered, her palm touching his chest. "Now tell me what happened."

Evan expelled a heavy breath and released her. "Canfield called me."

Morgan wrapped her arms around her waist and Evan saw fear flicker in her eyes. "Do you know where he was?" Her voice was calmly controlled, as if she was simply facing a reluctant witness rather than the threat to her life.

"Here." He paused. "He described the shirt you're wearing, at least the color."

Morgan shivered and Evan reached for her. She backed away with one hand held aloft. "Don't. I think I saw him."

Evan's blood ran cold. If the bastard touched her... "You think you saw him? Don't you remember what he looks like?"

"He's changed his looks, but when he laughed, I thought I recognized it. But then I thought I was just being paranoid." The look she gave Evan sent cold chills down his spine. "I guess I was wrong."

His temper roared to life. "What did he do to you?"

She shook her head almost viciously. "Nothing. He came to the door looking for Mrs. Eldridge. He said he was a friend of her son's. I told him I didn't know where she lived."

Clamping one hand around her wrist, he practically dragged her into the kitchen. "Sit." He jutted his chin toward a bar stool while he reached for the phone. It seemed to take forever for Shawn to answer the rings, and when he did, Evan revealed his displeasure by the shortness of his tone.

"Where in the hell have you been? You were supposed to be looking for Morgan."

"I was until I saw your truck barreling down the street. Figured you found her." Chadwick sounded defensive.

Evan forced himself to breathe. "Make sure next time. Now, I need you to check on Mrs. Eldridge. I saw her earlier in town, but go by her place and make sure everything's okay."

"Have you seen Canfield?"

"No. Got a call. He's here. Get back with me as soon as you make sure Marge is safe."

"Will do."

Ending the call, Evan hung up the receiver and dragged a shaking hand through his hair. "You know, I've been thinking." He turned to face Morgan. "Your parents will feel better if you were with them."

"I thought you were the one who wanted me to stay."

"I did. Long enough to set the trap. The bastard's here now. I can handle him."

"I'd feel better if you had an army backing you."

He walked toward her, stopping close enough for his hip to brush her knees. "I've handled serial killers before. Canfield won't leave this town without a body bag or handcuffs. I prefer a body bag."

She gave him a wobbly smile. "I'm not leaving."

"I could make you leave." He knew as soon as the threat left his lips he wouldn't make good on it. He wanted her nearby. He needed to be able to keep an eye on her and make sure Canfield didn't get wind of her departure and follow her. He gave himself an internal shake. Keeping her in Skyler might not be the safest course of action, but it was the best he could do for now.

Morgan broke into his reverie. "What are you thinking?"

He stuffed his hands in his pockets. "That this bastard is going to strike soon." His jaw tightened. "And we're in for a long night."

She squared her shoulders. "It's a good thing you said 'we' or you were going to have a problem." She slid down off the stool and bumped her forehead to his. "I survived his first attempt. I'll survive this time."

Evan yanked her into his arms again. "You're damned right, you will. You're damned right."

The alternative was unthinkable.

Ian banged on the screen door, stamping his boots to make his presence known.

Evan swung open the wooden door, his gun at the ready.

Ian held up his hand. "Jesus! Check the peephole, will ya?"

Jerking his head toward the living room, Evan stepped back and allowed the older man to enter. "I did, but I wasn't taking any chances."

The old man shuffled forward and swiped his cap off his head. "Look, I ain't gonna beat around the bush. I got wind of that call from the Tanners' neighbor, and with the way Shawn hauled ass over to Marge Eldridge's place, well, the whole town knows something is going on now. Don't you think you should be letting people know to be on the lookout? I mean if this bastard is amongst us," he paused to spit a stream of tobacco juice into the wastebasket, "then the citizens have a right to know."

"I'm not about to create widespread panic. Canfield is here for Morgan now. He's going to come after her."

"I guess he didn't realize Andrea wasn't Morgan," Ian returned in a snarky tone of voice.

Evan came around behind the sofa and shot a glance over his shoulder to make sure they were still alone. "Why don't you just say what you came here to say? But keep your voice down. I finally got Morgan to lie down for a while."

"You ain't got your head on straight right now. You're worried more about saving Morgan than you are about protecting the people you swore to protect. That ain't right."

Evan felt his stomach beginning to burn. "I'm doing my job."

"Yeah? Have you been out to see Andrea's family? Cause the last time we had a tragedy in this town, that's exactly what you did."

"Andrea's parents are dealing with a lot right now. They're spending every waking minute by their daughter's bedside in the hospital. If you're wondering how I know that, it's because I've been to the hospital."

Ian shrugged. "Okay. Fine. I was wrong, and I can admit when I'm wrong. But I ain't wrong about your warning the town. You need to let folks know they've got cause to worry. There's women walking these streets who don't know a killer is out there roaming around. Now, I'm taking Mae to her sister's house in Brevard, but I'm coming back because I think you're going to need some help."

Evan faced the older man with a calm expression. "I appreciate the offer, but it's probably best you stay with Mae. Things could get ugly here."

Ian stiffened, and Evan saw he'd hurt the man's feelings. "I spent four years in Vietnam, boy. Don't talk to me about ugly." He bobbed his head toward the door. "You're going to need more than just Chadwick to help you. Like I said, I'll be back."

Evan didn't figure he could stop him. And in truth, he probably would need all the help he could get.

Morgan stared at the phone as it rang, uncertain as to whether she should answer it. Could it be Dexter? He'd located Evan's cell phone number, so it wouldn't be unfeasible for him to discover the home phone number.

Her palms began to sweat, and just when she reached for the receiver, the shrilling stopped. She lifted her hair off the back of her neck and staggered toward the sofa. She didn't know how much more of this she could take.

The phone began to shrill again, and her heart slammed against her lungs. She covered her ears with her hands to try to drown out the noise, but it was a futile effort. She could hear each angry, demanding ring.

Shoving her fear aside, she clamped her hand around the receiver and brought it to her ear, battling back her terror.

"Do you know what happens when fire comes in contact with alcohol?"

Morgan came awake on a scream, her chest heaving, tears racing down her cheeks in rapid succession.

Evan barreled through the bedroom door, gun drawn, eyes wild. He assessed the situation in two seconds, holstered his gun and had her in his arms in three more. "It's okay. Baby, it's okay. I'm here. You're safe."

She clung to him, her nails sinking into his arms, but he didn't seem to notice the pain she inflicted. He just tightened his arms around her, pressing her head into his shoulder while he crooned to her.

"It was just a nightmare," he whispered next to her ear.

"It was so vivid," she responded, her voice breaking.

"You're safe. I won't let anything happen to you."

As much as she wanted to believe that, she wasn't so sure Evan would be able to stop Dexter.

"I want you to see something." Evan scooted off the bed and held out his hand.

Her legs shaking, she allowed herself to be led to the bedroom window.

"What do you see?"

"The lawn. The street. A battered pickup truck."

"Look closer. What do you see inside the pickup truck?"

Morgan squinted and leaned closer to the windowpane. "A man, but I don't recognize him."

"That would be Mike Harrigan. He's been deputized to keep an eye on this side of the house. I've got four more guys out there."

Her shoulders slumped. "They're civilians, Evan." She felt the need to remind him, even to warn him. "They're no match for Dexter."

Evan took hold of her shoulders. "Hold on a second. Mike isn't just a civilian. I only deputize men who've had combat training. Mike is a sharpshooter. He knows how to kill someone at five hundred yards. Rafe out back is former CIA and two more of the guys are Navy Seals. They've been in the line of fire before, and they know their business."

She relaxed only marginally. "When do you think he'll strike?" She hated the panicked sound to her voice, but her fears were rooted too deeply now. She saw danger around every corner and even the sound of the wind rustling the leaves outside the kitchen window had sent her into a moment of panic earlier.

"Probably at night fall, but if I play my cards right, that will give me plenty of time to finish what I started."

"Are you going to tell me this plan of yours?"

"Not yet." He ran his finger down the bridge of her nose. "But soon."

"Could you be more specific about the time?" she snapped.

His eyes settled on her face long enough to make her squirm. "Morgan, there's nothing you can do now. Let me do my job."

Her breath hissed out of her lungs. "Maybe I should leave, after all." Where had all her courage gone? Or maybe she hadn't really had it.

His hold on her gentled. "He'd only follow you. As much as I wanted to convince myself you'd be better off out of town, I knew Canfield wasn't going to give up that easily."

"Stop." She didn't want to hear anything else about how Dexter was calling the shots. "I should have stayed away. More and more people are getting hurt, Evan. I shouldn't be here."

"Morgan," his hand slid along her jaw, "you came back to Skyler for a reason."

She clutched at the soft cotton of his shirt. "You didn't exactly give me a choice."

"You didn't want one." His breath brushed over her face, warm and reassuring.

"So what exactly is this reason I'm supposed to have had?"

"Because you knew I could protect you. You trust me."

Releasing his shirt, Morgan walked to the edge of the bed and plopped down. "I'm scared." She hated admitting the words even more than the weakness in her limbs.

"I know, but I meant it when I said I won't let anything happen to you. Don't lose faith in me now."

She let out a shaky breath and even managed a laugh. "He's out there, Evan, and right now, all I can see is his face."

He moved to the bed and knelt down in front of her, taking her hands in his. "Then focus on mine. Listen to my voice. I will protect you. He won't hurt you again."

She closed her eyes, unable to speak. All she could do was pray that Evan was right.

And that he wouldn't die trying.

Dexter adjusted the collar of the starched white shirt and examined the gold stud in his left ear. He thought the earring made him look even more dangerous. He grinned at his reflection and gave himself a thumbs-up before turning away to reach for his suit coat.

The expensive wool caressed his shoulders and when he fastened the two buttons, he felt the material conform to his waist. Worth every penny of the twenty-five hundred he'd spent. Of course, he hadn't been spending his own money on the shopping spree so the excess really didn't matter.

The black calfskin "Park Avenues" provided the perfect match for his feet and when he added the gold cufflinks, he had to take another look. Perfect. He'd wanted to look his best for his next meeting with Morgan.

"I wonder if you recognized me, my sweet, when I stood outside Sheriff Hennessy's door." He chuckled. "You still looked the same. I'll bet you smelled the same, too." Tipping his head back, he sniffed the air. "God, incredible. I haven't forgotten your scent." He dipped his hand inside the front pocket of the coat and removed a sliver of lace which he brought to his nose and inhaled deeply. "I found this in your desk drawer, Morgan. Don't worry. I'll return it to you...when we meet again."

He returned the handkerchief to his pocket and sought the reassurance of his lighter. His fingers twirled the engraved piece of silver and he felt his blood pressure dropping.

"Now, off to meet the good citizens of Skyler, North Carolina."

Evan laid out the ground rules with clipped precision. No one would leave their post and they would check in every thirty minutes. The newly deputized men would each have partners and they were not to leave one another's sight. He stressed the importance of never lowering their guard.

He lifted his eyes and pinned the group with a serious stare. "This isn't a drill, guys. This guy means business. Mike, you and Jason round up the townspeople and get them into the storm shelter. It's the safest place."

"You really think the storm's going to be that bad?" Mike ducked his head to look out through one of the garage's tiny windows.

"It's not because of the storm. They'll be safer there than in their wooden houses."

Chadwick scuffed his feet against the tiled floor. They'd gathered in Evan's garage, as he refused to leave Morgan for more than a few minutes at a time. The deputy coughed, drawing all eyes to his reddening face.

"Something to say?" Evan sensed the man's discomfiture along with the next words.

"Don't you think it would be safer to just get Morgan out of town?"

A hush fell over the gathered group, and Evan heard bodies shifting and moving out of his way as he walked toward his deputy. He forced himself to remain calm, to understand where the deputy was coming from. "He'd only follow her."

Chadwick coughed and tugged at his collar. "But she wouldn't be here."

With fury born of fear, Evan's hands fisted in the deputy's collar and dragged him closer. "So that's it then? If we get her out of town, it's no longer our problem? Is that what you're thinking?"

Chadwick only struggled for a moment before meeting Evan's stare. "What I'm thinking right now is that you're taking too many chances to protect one woman. I'll bet you haven't even called the FBI. Don't you think they should be here? It's not just about protecting the woman you love, Evan. It's about protecting this town."

His hands unclenching, Evan gave the deputy a slight push backwards. "I've been in constant contact with the FBI since we were sure Canfield was close to the town. I just updated them an hour ago. A team is on its way in now."

A hand banged on the glass-plated door leading to the backyard before Ian stomped into the garage. "Holy Hell! That rain is really starting to come down out there. I got Mae to her sister's house just in time." He shook the wetness off his shoulders and dragged his cap from his head to thump it against his thigh. Then, as if taking stock of the silence, he peered over at the gathered group of men. "What's going on? It's as quiet as a funeral in here."

The men mumbled among themselves before Evan responded. "Are you here to work, Ian?"

The older man stood as tall as his bowed spine would allow. "Well, I damned sight ain't here for the company." He trudged toward the riding lawnmower. Parking his butt on the vinyl seat, he glared at the men. "Now, if someone will tell me what's going on here, I'd appreciate it."

"Evan called the FBI," Deputy Chadwick inserted, his eyes never leaving Evan's face.

Ian's eyes lit up. "Well, hot damn. When will the Calvary arrive?"

Evan walked around Ian and headed toward the door leading back into the house. "As soon as they can. Y'all have your assignments."

"Evan," Chadwick's voice croaked as he called out.

Without looking back, Evan continued into the house. He didn't want to hear an apology. Maybe that was wrong, but right now, if he continued a conversation with the deputy, it wouldn't have a pleasant ending. But then, he doubted tonight would have one anyway.

Morgan finished vacuuming and shook out the last of the rugs. She put on another load of laundry and began the task of scrubbing the kitchen from top to bottom, anything to stay busy.

In an effort to focus on the future, she'd called her former office and spoken with one of the partners. Instead of a welcome, she'd gotten the distinct impression she was neither wanted nor needed to return to her former position.

The call ended abruptly when the partner had taken an emergency call from Switzerland. Considering the time in Switzerland, Morgan doubted the veracity of the man's excuse. She'd let him go anyway. She'd already figured she would lose her job. Not that any of this was her fault, of course. Her mind quoted the partner's words. However, they had to maintain a certain image and tragedies of this nature left an unpalatable taste in the mouths of Raleigh's elite—translated, their clients.

She put more effort into scrubbing the counters than required, but she needed to vent her anger somewhere. She cursed herself for not seeing the signs long before her last day at Baker & Snyder. She made her living reading people and yet, she hadn't read Dexter.

Giving a little laugh, she added even more elbow grease to wipe the front of the stove. God knew Dexter had dropped enough clues. He'd constantly asked her to join him for dinner, and when she'd turned him down, preferring to keep their relationship professional, he seemed to accept her decision. But there'd always been something in his eyes, something she couldn't quite define.

She'd never understood why he'd continued to ask her out. Surely he expected the rejection, but perhaps the rejections only added to his arsenal of bitterness. She shivered as the icy blast from those pale, blue eyes shifted into her line of vision. She still saw those eyes in her sleep. Every night since her return to Skyler, the nightmares plagued her. Every night except for those she spent in Evan's arms.

Clutching the cleaning cloth in her hand, she sat at the kitchen table and recalled every sweet instance of the previous night. And afterwards, she'd fallen asleep in perfect peace. Her lips curved into a smile and when the phone rang, she didn't think twice about answering the summons. "Hello?"

"Morgan, how nice to hear your voice again."

The sinister words made her drop the receiver. Panic clawed at her insides as she righted the phone next to her ear. "Dexter." She should hang up, but her hand was frozen, holding desperately to the phone. "Why are you calling me?"

"You recognize my voice. I'm touched. Perhaps I should have used the accent again. Would you have recognized me then?" The laughter came again, chilling Morgan to the bone.

Her hands shook, but somehow, she found the strength to end the conversation really before it began. Reaching for the iron control that had carried her through many trials, she waited until Evan walked into the kitchen before she intoned, "He just called me."

Chapter Fourteen

Ian met Evan at the back door, his hat clutched in his hand. "Did I just hear the phone?"

"Yes," Evan growled, pushing his way past the old man as he lunged out into the garage. Pure adrenaline fueled his every move now. He had to take the upper hand again, force Canfield into thinking he was holding the ace.

Ian followed him. "I might be interested in what the call was about since it seems to have got you so riled up."

Evan didn't look behind him. "Canfield called her."

"She's gonna be okay, boy." The old man softened his voice.

Jaw clenched, Evan barely spared a look over his shoulder. "I wish I could be so sure of that."

"Well, hell, now, she don't need you to start doubting her safety."

Key in hand, Evan inserted it into the lock of a tall black locker. The door opened with a screech, revealing an arsenal of weapons and combat gear fit for an army.

"Now that looks like you're gearing up to fight ten Dexter Canfields."

"One is enough." He shrugged into a Kevlar vest and tightened it around his waist.

"You need to take some deep breaths, Evan. Think before you run off half-cocked."

Evan didn't acknowledge the words. "Why did you decide to come back instead of staying with Mae in Brevard?"

"I reckon I know what it's like to fear for someone you love."

Lifting a USAR_15A1 Assault Rifle from its hanger, Evan slipped it into the back sling and secured it in place. "This has nothing to do with love."

Ian gave a laugh that ended on a cough. "Sure it don't."

Evan lapsed into silence as he locked the fragmentation grenades onto his belt. Raising his hand, he captured a smoke grenade from the top shelf and attached it as well.

Feet scuffling on concrete, Ian peered over Evan's shoulder. "Ain't no shame in loving someone."

"See if my night visions are behind you."

"Jesus, are you going out after this guy?" Ian reached behind him on the lower shelf and retrieved a pair of goggles.

"Canfield's killed a lot of people."

"Going after him by yourself ain't going to save Morgan."

The knot in Evan's stomach grew in size, directly proportionate to the lump in his throat. "I'm not going to let this bastard get to her."

"Then you keep thinking that. I ain't never seen you lose yet and you've come up against some real tough asses in your day."

Evan silently admitted the truth behind Ian's words. His career had been peppered with hand-to-hand combat, taking down criminals with bad attitudes and lethal weapons. And somehow, Evan had managed to best them all. He just couldn't help wondering when his luck might run out.

Or even worse, when Morgan's would.

Weapons in place, he squatted down beside the ancient toolbox his father had left him. "I want you to take Morgan to the old bomb shelter as soon as I find the goddamned key. Stay there with her until I come for you."

"I don't think that's a good idea. The rain's starting to come down and any of us being out on the roads is exactly what that bastard is hoping for. He's just lying in wait, ready to spring like a coyote in a henhouse."

Evan didn't have time to argue. "Either you take her or I'll get Mike to do it, but she's going. It's the only place I know Canfield can't break into."

With a grumble, Ian clamped his cap back on his head. "Fine, but I just hope you know what you're doing."

Evan rested his hands on his thighs as he stared down at the tiny, silver key. "So do I."

Skyler, North Carolina reminded him of a ghost town. Apparently, the good sheriff had warned the citizens to stay behind locked doors. Dexter clicked his teeth as he strolled down Main Street. He inspected the fares inside the plate glass windows and took a longer amount of time perusing the bakery's wares before finally moving on.

It seemed odd to him that no cars rolled by, not even a patrol car. He grinned to himself. The entire police department was probably huddled outside of Sheriff Hennessy's house. Dumb bastards.

The rain began again, first coming down in tiny dribbles before the bottom of the sky fell out. Dexter snapped open his black umbrella and warded off the torrents. He picked a hell of a time to arrive in the little country town.

How exactly was he supposed to set anything ablaze in the rain?

Evan snagged the black bag out from under his bed while Morgan stood in the doorway of his bedroom, hands clamped on her hips.

"I'm not going anywhere."

"The hell you aren't." Evan disappeared into the adjoining bathroom, returning with a handful of linens and a bar of soap. "The bomb shelter has a pump in it so you'll have access to water. Ian is grabbing some food from the cabinets." He walked around the bed and flicked her a glance. "You'll stay there until you hear from me. Ian is taking a two-way radio but only use it in an emergency. The waves can be traced."

Morgan practically stamped her foot. "Evan, you're not listening to me. I'm not going anywhere."

He stopped packing the bag long enough to glance over his shoulder. "This isn't up for discussion, Morgan. You're going and that's final."

"If I'd known you were going to ship me off, I might as well have gone with my parents."

He approached her, a small pistol nestled in his palm. "Take this with you and pray you don't have to use it."

Morgan's gaze fell to the weapon before winging back up to Evan's face. "And what are you going to be doing while I'm cowering in fear?"

She watched a muscle tic in Evan's cheek as he zipped the bag. "You're not cowering. I have to make sure you're safe so I can focus on taking Dexter down."

"I can help you."

He settled his hands on her shoulders. "You can help me by going to the bomb shelter without any more bitching."

She jerked out of his embrace and reached for the bag, tugging the strap over her shoulder. "Fine. I'll hide, but Dexter isn't as stupid as you give him credit."

Evan swatted her on the butt. "I'll take my chances."

Ian kept his hand tight around the back of Morgan's arm while he hustled her forward. Ducking his head against the onslaught of rain, he kept the semi-automatic straight ahead, looking for trouble.

The howl of the wind made it almost impossible to hear anything, including following footsteps, but Morgan swore she heard them anyway. The crunch of the leaves and the howling of a lone dog in the distance made her shiver inside Evan's thick, leather jacket.

The umbrella wobbled overhead and she tightened her hand around the thick, wooden knob. "How much farther?" she shouted over the screeching wind.

Ian pointed with one finger and stumbled forward. "Right around the next bend. Now, keep your voice down. We don't want to alert this bastard." He quickened the pace, his fingers digging into her wrist.

Through the heavy downpour, Morgan could make out a wooden door with rusty hinges set back in a hill.

Ian chugged ahead and inserted the key in the heavy padlock. The door screeched and protested as he pulled it open and a cloud of dust puffed out into the rain.

"Home sweet home," he muttered, stepping back to allow Morgan to go ahead of him. "Take the stairs carefully. I'll be right behind you with the flashlight."

Her heart in her throat, Morgan followed his command, her muscles tense and instincts telling her Dexter wouldn't be so easily fooled. But all she could do was pray Evan would be all right and that he would come for her soon.

Evan tugged the stocking cap low over his ears. Knowing Dexter still roamed the streets of Skyler meant he'd have to get out in the thick of things. The son-of-a-bitch had every intention of luring him out into the midst.

And Evan would oblige him.

He ripped open the front door just as the electricity died. He stood there for a long moment in the silence, long enough to smell the thick, acrid scent of smoke.

Ian was on the lookout, but Evan still caught him by surprise as he came to the door of the fallout shelter.

"Jesus!" Ian snapped, clutching the handgun close to his chest. "I could have shot your ass!"

Evan shoved him inside the shelter. "But you didn't. How's Morgan?"

"She's nervous as hell. What did you expect? What are you doing here anyway? I thought you weren't going to come here until you'd caught the bastard."

Evan clamped a hand on Ian's shoulder. "He pulled a trump card I wasn't counting on." He lowered his voice. "He set fire to my house."

Dexter adjusted his gloves and surveyed his handiwork. Not much of a fire, but definitely a good deal of smoke. Not too shabby, though. Definitely enough to send Evan Hennessy on the run.

Smiling gleefully, he strolled around the house, tugging the baseball cap low on his head. Now just to follow them as they fled the house. Hennessy was bound to lead him straight to Morgan.

Apparently, this Evan fella wasn't as smart as he thought he was. Dumb bastard. Dexter would make sure he was the first to go when he caught up with them. He wanted to take his sweet time with Morgan.

A sweet, very long time.

"Wake up, bitch. I've been looking for you for a long, long time."

The words reached out to her, enshrouding her in the terrifying images of the past. She shook her head almost violently, but a hand dipped from the shadows and caught hold of her hair. She gave a yelp of pain.

"I said, wake up, or don't you listen?"

"I don't want to wake up," she whispered. She felt his hot breath brushing her cheek and she recoiled, shrinking against the couch. "Leave me alone."

He stroked his fingertips down her neck before lightly caressing the sloped line of her blouse. "Have I ever told you how beautiful you are, Morgan? No, I don't think I have. That's probably because you never gave me the chance." His voice hardened and he dragged her closer by her hair. "You were too good for me, weren't you?"

Tears stung her eyelids, but Morgan didn't open her eyes. She didn't want to see Dexter's face. She opened her mouth to cry for Evan, but no words would come.

Then Dexter began shaking her. "Wake up, I said. Wake up!"

Evan knelt down beside Morgan, running his hand up and down her arm. "Morgan, I need you to wake up, honey. You're okay. I'm here."

Her eyes popped open. "Is it over?" She pushed her back up against the wall of rock. "Did you get him?"

Evan shook his head slowly. "Not yet. I'm going back out in a minute, but I just wanted to make sure you were all right."

She clutched at his arms. "He's out there. I could feel him."

He bumped his forehead to hers. "I know, but you're going to be safe."

She scooted closer to the warmth of his body. "Do you have to leave just yet?"

He settled down next to her and wrapped his arm around her. "I think I can spare a few minutes."

Morgan rested her head on his shoulder. "Can we talk?"

He cupped her cheek. "What do you want to talk about?"

"Anything but what's outside."

Evan kissed the top of her head and Morgan felt her muscles unfurling. "We can talk about anything you want to talk about."

Her head popped up so suddenly she narrowly missed his chin. "Why are you being so accommodating?"

He tweaked her nose. "Why are you being so paranoid?"

"Oh, I don't know. Maybe it's because I'm being stalked by a psychopath."

"I thought you wanted to talk about something else."

Her lips pulled into a smile. "You've got me there."

His fingers began to trail up and down her arm. "Did you have a subject in mind?" The lantern overhead swayed, throwing shadows across the hard lines of his face and highlighting his sensual lips.

Morgan nestled her head against his shoulder again. "Have you dated anyone?"

His hand stilled. "When?"

"Since we've been divorced."

The stroking resumed. "Not really."

"It's a yes or no question, Evan."

He fell silent for a long moment before finally responding. "I've gone out with a group of people and members of that group have tried to set me up with someone who tagged along. It never worked." He cleared his throat. "So why have you never settled down with another guy?"

Morgan hedged. "Another guy?"

"Nice evasive tactic, Counselor."

"Thanks. It's a class we take in law school. Evasive Maneuvers 101."

His chest shook with his laughter. "I'll bet you passed that one."

She chuckled, but a thump on the outer door ended her mirth abruptly.

Evan shot to his feet, his semi-automatic clearing the holster at his side in one swift movement. He pressed a finger to his lips as an indication for silence and crept slowly toward the door.

Morgan drew her feet up underneath her and bit down hard on her hand. Every muscle in her body craved release, but she couldn't move. "What is it?" she finally asked when she couldn't stand the suspense any longer.

He gave her a hard look over his shoulder and emphasized the need for silence again. Peeking out the peephole, he raised his hand to release the lock. Morgan's horrified breath made him pause, and he turned toward her slowly. "I can't see Ian so I have to check out the noise. I want you to stay put. Don't go outside."

"What do you think it is?" she whispered.

"I'm not sure. Now just do as I tell you to do."

For once, she didn't protest his authority. She bobbed her head and drew her legs up to her chest, lowering her head to her knees, praying for safety, for Evan's safety, for life.

Evan heard Ian's approach and though he wondered if the old man could hold his own, he didn't have time to ask. He simply waved Ian across the valley and held the lantern higher. His breaths fogged in the air, and his heart thumped wildly against his chest.

A flash of lightning illuminated the damp ground at his feet. Holding tightly to caution, he moved further outside, his gun at the ready. A movement captured his eye and he spun and took aim. "Freeze!"

"Don't shoot," came the croaking response.

Evan leveled his weapon. "Who are you?"

The man staggered into view, his face beaten and bloody. Evan managed to capture the guy before he could fall down.

"Tell me who you are. Who did this to you?"

"It's-it's Mike, Evan."

Mike sat on the floor of the bomb shelter while Ian treated his injuries. Evan paced back and forth in front of the back door.

"How could you let the bastard get that close to you?" Evan bit out the words.

"I've already told you! I didn't see him," Mike shot back, wincing as Ian doused a cut next to his lip with alcohol.

"What? Is the guy a friggin' ghost?"

Ian held up one hand. "Ain't gonna do no good to start fightin'. This Canfield fella thinks he's calling all the shots."

Evan dropped down to the ground opposite Mike. "Right now he is." He lowered his weapon to his thigh and sank his head into his hands.

"And you're not going to be able to stop him," Morgan said in such a quiet tone of voice Evan spun around.

"We have to move. Mike probably led Canfield right to us."

Morgan came forward and laid her hand on Mike's shoulder. "I'm sorry. This wasn't supposed to happen." She didn't appear concerned or scared at the state of affairs.

The veteran looked up at her. "I knew when I signed on for this job this was a possibility. You take the good with the bad."

Evan exhaled loudly and gripped Morgan's arm. "Come with me."

She didn't fight him as he propelled her farther into the bomb shelter. He didn't stop walking until he reached another door, just as creaky as the first one. He flashed his light out over the grassy knoll. "I want you to stay by this door. If you hear me shout, go out this door and run like hell. Do you understand me? Don't stop running. I will catch up with you."

Morgan's eyes widened and she gripped the lapels of his shirt. "You're leaving me?"

"Only for a little while. Ian and Mike will stay at the front of the shelter. Dexter will have to get through them first."

"Mike is in no shape to defend himself."

Evan kissed her hard. "You let me worry about the front line. Just do as I ask, okay."

"Evan." She grasped his hand before he could pull away from her. He stopped, eyebrows lifted, waiting for her to say what she needed to say.

"Be careful. I don't want to lose you."

He paused, his hazel eyes filling with warmth. "You're not going to lose me. In fact, once this is all over, you're going to wonder how in the hell you lived without me."

She managed a wobbly smile. "Just watch your back."

Another kiss was his only response before he slipped out the back door into the pouring rain.

Evan raced up the hill and made it to the top just as his cell phone trilled. Tingles of awareness raced up his spine and he knew even before answering who his caller was. "I'm giving you until dawn to turn yourself in or I'm coming after you." He lied smoothly. Time to put the snake on the defensive.

Canfield broke out into gales of laughter. "Sounds a little desperate, Sheriff. Why are you being so magnanimous? Don't you want me to turn myself in now to save your town?"

"I'll save my town. I'm giving you a warning. Turn yourself in and live, at least for a little while longer, or make me come after you, and I'll put you in a body bag."

"You sound like you didn't like the little present I gave your bodyguard." Canfield clicked his tongue against his teeth. "The guy wasn't too up on his job. He didn't even see me coming."

Evan clenched his teeth. "Don't think you have the upper hand."

"Don't I?"

The touch of cold steel in his hand reassured him. "That's when people make mistakes."

"Haven't you heard? I don't make mistakes."

Evan chuckled, though he wanted to reach through the phone and wrap his fingers around Canfield's throat. "I guess we'll see then. Have a good evening."

"You're going to hang up before you trace me?" Canfield's voice held disbelief.

"You really have been out of the loop, haven't you? We have other ways of tracking criminals. Better ways. I hope you're not afraid of needles, Canfield. The State of North Carolina is going to take great pride in executing you." Evan clicked the phone shut, refusing to waste one more second of his time on a lost cause.

Dexter hung the suit back in the closet and stepped out of the expensive loafers. He'd spent too much time out in the rain with them and now, the calfskin looked a little worse for wear. He placed them next to the vent in hopes the air would help dry them out.

His knuckles ached, but for a good cause. He'd given that special deputy some scars he wouldn't soon forget. Dexter chuckled at his own abilities. The bastard never even saw him coming. That was precisely the way he liked it.

The television held little interest for him except for a news story out of Raleigh. The FBI was now involved in the massive manhunt for a crazed serial killer, Dexter Canfield. His visage was splayed across the screen and Dexter pursed his lips.

"I look better in real life. Never was photogenic." He switched off the tube and retrieved a beer from the small fridge at the foot of the bed. For such a dump, the motel had thought of everything.

Flopping down on the bed, he stacked several pillows behind his back and took leisurely sips of the strong brew. He conjured images of Morgan in a long, flowing white dress walking toward him, her face scrubbed free of make-up. Through the thin material, he could see the perky tips of her breasts and his breaths became shorter.

She was exquisite. So vibrantly beautiful and real. He wanted to claim her for his own, but knew she would resist. He wanted a woman who wanted him and only him, but Evan Hennessy had gotten to Morgan first, had ruined her for any other man. Even years after their divorce, Morgan still pined for him.

Dexter's legs scissored on the mattress and frustration mounted. He'd asked her out time and again, only to rebuffed in a polite, yet firm manner. He'd cajoled, and almost resorted to pleading, but still she turned him away. The night before the fire, he'd reached his limit.

She'd left the door to her office ajar and he'd watched her. He'd lost track of time as she read through a thick, manila file, occasionally stopping to adjust her glasses or take a sip of the hot tea she liked. She'd leaned back in the leather chair and propped her feet on the edge of her desk and her tight, blue had ridden on her thighs.

Dexter's hands clenched into fists as he recalled the painful amount of courage it had taken for him to push open the door of her office with a light tap against the buffed wood. She'd looked up, but instead of a welcome in her eyes, he'd seen annoyance before she'd quickly removed all traces from her face.

She'd slipped her feet off the desk and tugged her skirt down closer to her knees while pasting one of her patented, courteous smiles on her lips.

Dexter almost lost his courage then, but he'd walked farther into the room anyway. He'd asked her to join him in some takeout and the irritation climbed back into those wickedly sexy green eyes. Even before she'd voiced her refusal, she'd rejected him for the final time. When he left her office that night, he knew then what he had to do.

He'd always hated uppity women, women who thought they were better than he was. He had a law degree, had worked his ass off to cheat his way to a higher degree of education and what had it gotten him? Rejection from classier women.

He twisted to his side and set the beer bottle onto the table next to the bed. "Morgan, why couldn't you have liked me?" As he said the words aloud, he knew. Evan Hennessy. Morgan would never love a man like she loved him. Dexter had seen it in her eyes each time she'd mentioned his name, and his name came up more often than it should.

Dexter had questioned her about that once and had gotten an icy stare in response. Then, he'd backed off, but the morning after Morgan's last refusal, the clichéd straw, he didn't back off.

He pushed himself to a sitting position and rubbed his hands together. He'd considered shooting her, but what better way to put a spoiled prima donna in her place than to take away that which she coveted the most? He'd never intended to kill her...at least not at first. But the fire had gotten out of hand and Morgan's screams and the sprinkler system had alerted the entire building. He'd barely managed to escape before security had arrived on the scene.

Dexter grinned to himself and pushed off the bed, stretching his arms wide.

"But I always finish what I start."

Chapter Fifteen

The alarm sounded at precisely two a.m. Dexter rolled and punched the snooze button on the dime store clock and stretched his arms over his head.

Anticipation pumped through his veins, driving him from the warmth of the bed and straight into the shower. His blood hummed as he stood beneath the pounding spray and he practically danced with excitement.

The citizens who'd chosen to remain behind in Skyler, North Carolina, were about to get a very rude awakening.

Evan crouched low in the darkness, the collar of his shirt turned up to ward off the chill of the biting rain. His feet sank into the damp earth as he hunkered on the bridge overlooking the town of Skyler. From the vantage point, he could see every move any citizen made...or any stranger.

Adjusting the scope of his high-powered rifle, he settled the target against his eye. So far, nothing moved. The town remained silent, hidden behind closed doors, heeding his warning.

A movement next to the front door of the library caught his attention, and Evan sat up straighter. A stray dog sniffed for food next to the glass doors and his shoulders relaxed.

"Sheriff, are you there?" Deputy Chadwick's ominous tone squawked across the two-way radio.

Evan responded to the call with a clipped, "What is it?"

"It's not something I want to tell you over the phone, sir. Just come to the hardware store."

As the deputy disconnected the call, a sick feeling settled inside of Evan's stomach. Edgar Blakely, the owner of Blakely Hardware, had been one of the citizens who'd refused to join the others in the storm shelter.

It took Evan less than five minutes to reach the hardware store and two more to whirl away from the grotesque picture of Edgar Blakely's last few minutes on earth.

"Cut him down," Evan instructed curtly, turning his back on Edgar's swinging body.

Chadwick fell into step beside him. "You want me to go talk to his wife."

Evan battled back the red haze stealing his vision. "No, I'll do it. You just get him to the coroner's office and make sure no one else sees him like that."

"I'd doubt they'd recognize him anyway." The deputy shuddered.

Evan didn't respond as he walked away, but he agreed. Canfield knew fire, and the burns covering Edgar Blakely's body would prevent a positive identification. Fury coursed through his veins as he stormed back toward his truck. He climbed into the driver's seat and dropped his head to the steering wheel.

Canfield really was as good as Morgan feared.

Evan made his way back to the shelter, erasing his tracks as he traveled, not that Dexter didn't already know where the shelter was. Odds were good Canfield had followed Mike.

Which left Evan wondering why the asshole hadn't struck yet. Instincts told him Dexter was waiting for a screw-up, an opening where he could slip right in and take Morgan without having to deal with more than one person at a time.

Evan tapped once on the wooden door and Ian opened it with a grumble.

"Where in the hell have you been? I was starting to get a little spooked."

Evan pushed past him. "Edgar Blakely is dead."

Ian spat out a curse and whirled. "This fella is starting to get on my last nerve." Bony fingers scratched his head. "You really think the guy's gonna come here? I'd think he wouldn't come so close, especially where there are three of us here to watch over Morgan while the other two deputies are still roaming the streets."

"He'll come." Evan tucked a string of wire into the crevice between the door and concrete underneath. He jerked his head toward the back of the shelter. "How's Morgan?"

"She's antsy. I checked on her about five minutes ago, and she was pacing."

Evan tucked the last bit of the wire around the front door and straightened. "I'm going to go check on her. She must be going crazy."

He found her crouched by the back door of the shelter, the small pistol clutched in her palm like a lifeline.

"Morgan?" He made sure his voice was soft, reassuring.

Morgan lowered the gun only marginally. "Have you found him yet?"

He squatted down beside her, his hand at the small of her back. "He'll find us."

"And that's what you want him to do?" She gave him a surprised look while she nibbled on her lower lip.

He stroked her arm. "That's what he has to do." He touched his lips to hers. "I'll do what I can to keep you from coming face to face with him."

Morgan shook her head mutinously and her hand tightened around the handle of the pistol. "Maybe I need to see him again, Evan." Her voice was dull, almost disheartened.

"And then what are you going to do once you see him?"

Uncertainty flickered in her eyes, but Morgan held her ground. "Kill him."

Evan took hold of her shoulders and met her gaze. "Have you ever killed someone, Morgan?" He asked the question even though he knew the answer. "Have you ever pointed a weapon at someone and pulled the trigger, knowing that bullet would end their life?" He saw her swallow hard and he gently eased the gun out of her hands. "You can't track Canfield down because you're not a killer. You're not trained to hunt people."

Her teeth worried her lower lip, and he wondered if she was even listening to him.

"I don't remember telling you we couldn't find Dexter Canfield. It's just much easier to let him come to us. He'll be in our backyard where I call the shots. It's leveling the playing field." He cupped her face. "And I need you to trust me."

She leaned her forehead against his. "I do trust you."

He kissed her nose then her lips. "Good. Then know that I will do my job no matter what it takes."

Her breath whooshed out in a long stream of air. "I just don't want you to get hurt."

Evan managed a laugh and pulled her into his arms. "I've been hurt before, Morgan. I'm tougher than I look. Look," he slid his hands up and down her spine, "I know this is difficult for you."

She broke free of his embrace and climbed to her feet. "I don't doubt you know the difficulty, but I can't help but wonder if this has become some sort of game to you. You've told me many times about the war games while you were in the Seals and the celebrations which took place after you always captured your man. I just hope that's not what you're thinking now."

Evan's temper soared and he walked closer to come eye to eye with her. "I don't know where that came from, but you couldn't be farther off the mark."

She wrapped her arms around her waist. "I'm sorry. I shouldn't have said that."

"You've never hidden your feelings from me, Morgan. I don't expect you to start now." He drew her close against his chest, wrapping his arms around her. "Once upon a time, we could tell each other everything."

"Once upon a time we were married."

He rested his chin atop her head. "Our divorce didn't change my feelings for you."

She curved her fingers over the top of his hands. "He's out there, Evan. Waiting for us to make a mistake. And then I'll come face to face with him again."

His arms tightened. "You won't face him alone. I promise you that."

Her shoulders shook a little. "What happened to us?"

"Like I said before, I think we both got tired of trying." It was the first answer he could come up with. In reality, he wasn't sure what had ended their marriage. He knew he'd never stopped loving her and probably never would, which was exactly why he'd never really gotten around to dating again. He just wasn't interested in anyone else.

She turned in his arms, resting her forehead against his chest. "I wish..." She grew silent.

"What do you wish?" He tipped her chin up to see his face. "Tell me."

"Nothing. It's nothing that we should be talking about now."

"Dammit, Morgan. We're not going to get anywhere if we aren't honest with each other."

Her eyes flashed. "Honesty? Is that what you're looking for?" Pulling out of his embrace, she walked around him. "I can give you honesty, Evan. I love you." Her breath caught in her throat. "I have always loved you, but it was never enough for you."

"Never enough? What in the hell are you talking about?" He gripped her shoulders. "Don't you know how much I loved you, still love you?"

Tears filled her eyes and she looked down at the dirt floor. "So why did we get tired of trying if we both loved each other so much?"

Evan drew in a deep breath, inhaling the scent of her hair, her skin. The softness of her fingers rested against his forearms, tantalizing him. "I'm not sure."

Silence fell for a long moment then Morgan finally spoke again.

"I can't go through this again."

"Go through what?"

"Opening my heart to you again only to risk losing it. When I left you, I thought I would never survive it."

Fury clawed at his insides. "No one told you to leave."

She pushed against his chest. "No, you didn't tell me to leave, but you didn't ask me to stay, either."

"For God's sake, Morgan, I had a job to do."

"Which was considerably more important than your family." Her breaths came in short gasps, her eyes flashing with her anger. "I wanted more with you, more than you were willing to give. Each time I brought up children, you panicked."

He gritted his teeth. "I didn't panic, but I didn't think we were ready." He paused. "I wasn't ready."

"And that was most important, wasn't it? That you be ready. Never mind whether or not I was." Her shoulders hunched and she turned away from him. "Never mind, this isn't getting us anywhere."

Evan pulled in a deep breath and crammed his hands into the pockets of his jeans. "Are you still ready?"

She pressed her palm against the rough wooden door. "What are you asking?"

"We're still connected." He didn't move toward her though he desperately wanted to take her in his arms. The need to hold her overwhelmed him, dragged him under. He hungered for her. Could she feel it?

She remained silent for so long he wondered if she was even going to respond. He heard the rustle of her blouse against her shoulders, the whisper of her hair and the soft breaths she drew in.

And he wanted her. Desperately.

"Morgan?" He finally broke the silence, his voice thick in the inky blackness.

She held up one hand to stop him. "I can't do this right now. I've loved you for so long and now, I..." She broke off, her voice thick with tears.

He came to stand behind her, but he kept his hands to himself. "Then don't give up on us yet."

When she didn't respond, Evan walked to the door, pausing to add over his shoulder, "We can talk more about this later, but for now, I have an animal to trap."

He didn't look back as he left her, but he hoped she would look back. And remember how much they loved one another.

And how strong their marriage had been once.

Chapter Sixteen

He smelled victory, but most importantly, he smelled Morgan. The sweet, flowery scent of her perfume and the heady aroma of her shampoo. Every muscle in his body tensed and he flicked the lighter in the front pocket of his slacks.

It was time to finish the job he'd started in Raleigh. "Sweet, sweet Morgan. I can't wait to see you again."

She counted her own breaths as the air grew thick around her. With each ticking of the second hand on her watch, she waited for Canfield's arrival. She knew he'd come. Any second now, she'd be face to face with him again. Though Evan told her to stay by the back door, she couldn't stand still. Panic drove her forward.

Her hand shook as she brought the pistol eye level. Could she pull the trigger when she saw his pale, blue eyes? No, she'd never killed a man before, but could she make an exception?

Her lungs ached and her muscles quivered as she returned to the back door of the shelter. She smelled the earth closing in around her and heard the dripping of a small trickle of water behind her.

Every sound seemed to echo, growing louder and louder, trying to drown out the sounds of her own attempts to remain calm.

She couldn't see the face of her watch, but she knew it must be closing in on dawn. Evan was sure Dexter would strike before then.

She listened to the sound of the rain soaking the earth. Occasionally, a flash of lightning illuminated the dirt floor, only heightening the tension.

The aged door creaked, and her heart beat a frantic rhythm. "It's just nerves, Morgan. Just nerves." The self-talk didn't work.

And as she looked up, the door began to open.

A scream bubbled in Morgan's throat as skinned knuckles came into view. The hand pulled the door open wider, and a shadowy figure filled the doorway.

"Hello, Morgan."

The voice washed over her, weakening her knees as fear squeezed her heart.

Dexter Canfield.

"I'll bet you never expected to see me again." Chortling at his own humor, Dexter strolled into the shelter, his beady eyes scanning the darkness. "I take it you're alone."

Morgan couldn't answer. A lump lodged in her throat and her mouth worked to form a sentence.

He walked closer and his cologne wafted over her, sickeningly sweet and cloying. Horror shimmied its way down her spine.

"My sweet, sweet, Morgan."

She edged her hand into the waistband of her jeans and felt the reassurance of the pistol. She wasn't a victim this time. She had protection. Her teeth chattered, but she quickly stifled the sound.

"Have you been waiting for me long?"

Morgan swallowed hard. She couldn't think and the panic in her voice only made Dexter's smile broaden.

"Do I frighten you, my sweet?"

Tremors raced down her spine. She couldn't do this. No one could fight Dexter Canfield and win. He was invincible. Unstoppable.

And he would win.

Morgan's courage wavered, but she withdrew the gun from her waistband and aimed it at Dexter's stomach.

"Whoa! What is this?" He smirked at her, flicking a dismissing gaze toward the pistol. "Do you really think you have the guts to shoot me, Morgan?" Clamping his hands on his hips, he raked his eyes up and down her shaking body. "Then go ahead." He held his arms away from his waist. "Pull the trigger."

Her hands wobbled, but she held the gun aloft. "Don't think I won't, Dexter."

He folded his arms across his chest. "I don't think you will. You see, I know you. I know you intimately, and women like you don't have the guts to pull the trigger. You could never kill, not even to protect your own life. You're that insipid."

His words served to spur her purpose, and she cocked the trigger on the pistol and leveled it. "You're mistaken. I will kill you and I won't think twice about it." But she knew even as she said the words that she was lying. She wasn't sure she could shoot Dexter, even if it meant saving her own life. To watch a man die at her own hands would take more courage than she had within her.

Sobbing silently, she took several steps backwards until her spine connected with the stone wall behind her. She kept holding the gun up to ward Dexter off. She saw his hand go into the pocket of his jacket, and her blood ran cold.

He retrieved the lighter with a flourish, brandishing it for her inspection. "Remember this, my sweet?" He flicked the switch, and the small flame ignited, riveting Morgan's eyes.

Her breath staggered in her throat, and her knees bumped against one another. She couldn't move, could barely think and when Dexter came closer, for a moment, she feared she wouldn't be able to pull the trigger.

But then he touched her, and she squeezed.

The report of the bullet brought Evan up short and he stopped in his tracks and listened. The scream which followed spurred him onward. He recognized Morgan's voice.

Terror lending wings to his feet, he burst through the bushes and barreled toward the back door of the shelter. He knew without a doubt that somehow Canfield had managed to find the back door even through the maze of tree limbs and bushes. And before Evan's hand closed around the handle, he knew the bastard was inside.

"Evan!" Morgan screamed just as he flung the door open wide.

Dexter knelt on the floor, one hand holding the top of his thigh. "The bitch shot me!"

Evan took aim, the barrel directed between Canfield's eyes. "Morgan, are you all right?"

She clutched the pistol to her chest and nodded.

Evan held out his hand. "I want you to give me the gun, honey." From the glazed look in her eyes, he saw that she was seconds away from snapping. The last thing she needed was a gun in her hand.

Morgan looked down at the barrel of the pistol, confusion etched on her face. "He had the lighter."

"I know, baby, but I've got him." Evan focused his attention on Canfield's kneeling form. "Where's the lighter?"

Dexter chuckled, sinister and coy. "Do you really think I would give up my only chance at freedom?" He pushed himself to his feet, and Evan immediately assumed a fighting stance.

"Did you think I would beg for my life?" Dexter queried in a slightly bored tone of voice.

Evan watched his every move, anticipating a rat's attempt to break out of the maze. "I don't expect you to do anything but sit behind bars for the rest of your life."

Dexter clicked his tongue. "I cannot begin to tell you how unpalatable that sounds. No, I don't think I'm going to be able to assist you with that. In fact, I have a better idea."

"Evan, look out!" Morgan took aim with the pistol again.

"Morgan, don't!" Evan braced himself for Dexter's attack, but the man surprised him by dropping to his knees, his hands clasped together in front of him. "What in the hell are you doing?"

Dexter lowered his head. "I don't want to die. Promise me if I go quietly, you won't kill me."

Instincts screamed loud and long. "Get up on your feet." Evan toed the man's leg.

Canfield turned, still on his knees. "Please promise me."

Evan palmed the semi-automatic. "I'll promise you nothing. Now, get your ass up before I put a bullet between your eyes."

"I know you hate me," Dexter's voice sounded muffled.

"Yeah, you're right. I hate you, and I'd give my right arm to be able to pull this trigger. But I obey the law. You'll go to prison, and God willing, the state will kill you."

Canfield's shoulders hunched, and he shook his head. "I don't think I could make it in there."

"I'm not worried about what you can or can't do."

"You hate me because I hurt Morgan," Dexter whined.

Hate seemed so mild of a word now that Evan stood looking down at the man who'd tortured Morgan. He abhorred everything about the bastard, wanted to see him dead, but even more, he wanted to spit on the son-of-a-bitch's grave.

"I hate you because you're useless," Evan returned in a harsh tone of voice.

Dexter responded with a crude comment, and Evan poked him with his toe again.

"I'm going to count to three, Canfield, and if your ass isn't up off the ground, I'm going to shoot you where you kneel."

Dexter looked up and Evan noticed his bulging cheeks and the gleam in his eyes as he brought the lighter up to his lips. Without second thought, Evan pulled the trigger.

The report of the bullet echoed across the mountainside, disturbing the night animals. As Canfield tumbled to one side, Evan approached him cautiously, assuring himself that the bastard was, indeed, dead before he put his weapon away.

"He's dead," he whispered, whipping his gaze to Morgan's face.

She stared back at him. "He's dead?"

"Yeah. This time, he's not coming back."

Morgan fisted her hand against her mouth and stumbled toward Evan. "I shot him."

He wrapped his arms around her. "You only nicked him. You didn't kill him, Morgan."

"I was aiming for his crotch."

Evan winced and held her tighter. "Your aim was off." He rested his chin atop her head and held her trembling body against his. "It's over, baby. It's all over."

Red and blue lights illuminated the night and Evan wrapped one arm around her waist. "We'd better get out of here. You need a long, hot bath and a good night's rest." He saw by the flutter of her eyelashes that Morgan relished the offer.

He led her out into the darkness, tucked her in the backseat of an unmarked patrol car and checked in with Chadwick before he commandeered the vehicle. "Ian and Mike are cleaning things up at the hardware store. Jason's gone to the shelter to let folks know it's safe to go back home."

Evan clamped a hand on his shoulder. "Thanks."

Chadwick nodded. "Can I ask you one thing, Sheriff?"

"Yeah."

"Did you really think we'd win?"

Evan dropped his hand. "We didn't have a choice. A lot of people depended on us." He looked back toward the car where Morgan sat with her head bowed. "Special people. Once you wrap things up here, head on home. I'll call the FBI and let him know we've got the bastard."

Chadwick scrubbed the back of his neck and shifted from one foot to the other. "Yeah, okay. Evan, look. Back there at your house—"

"Don't. There's no need. All of us were worried. There was a lot at stake."

"Thanks, Sheriff." The deputy lightly punched Evan's arm before backing away. "I'll see you tomorrow, then?"

"Actually, I think I might be taking tomorrow off."

The hot, scented water felt like heaven as it settled around her shoulders, soothing her muscles and warming away the tension.

Morgan lay back against the satin pillow and closed her eyes. And for the first time in a very long time, she didn't see Dexter Canfield's face.

A relieved sigh escaped her lips and she scooted the headphones into place. Since Dexter had set fire to Evan's house, Evan had rented a room in the local bed and breakfast and now, she was enjoying the benefits of the luxury.

The claw-footed bathtub stood in the center of a marble bathroom and fluffy, white towels hung from pewter hooks, inviting their warmth.

Morgan never wanted to leave the heat, but all too soon, the water cooled and she forced herself to climb out of the liquid cocoon. Wrapping herself in the thick terrycloth robe she'd found hanging on the back of the door, she secured her hair in a towel and brushed her teeth.

It took her a few moments to realize the different feeling awakening within her. She felt...safe.

The doorknob turned and Evan stood in the doorway, a worried expression on his face. "I just thought I'd come to check on you. You've been in here a while."

Morgan looked at her reflection in the mirror. "I know. I'm sorry."

He came to stand behind her. "I wasn't complaining. Just checking."

She pinched her cheeks to add a little color. "Thank you, Evan."

He frowned. "For what?"

"For saving my life."

"You had just as much to do with that as I did."

She doubted that, but she didn't want to argue tonight. In fact, tonight, she had other plans in mind. Plans which involved the use of the canopied bed in the center of the luxurious suite just off the bathroom.

He settled his hands on her shoulders. "Are you feeling better?"

"Mmm, much," she agreed, pressing her back against his chest. "Thank you."

He began to massage the muscles in her neck. "You're still tight."

"Maybe I need a full massage," she suggested with a slight, breathless quality to her voice.

Evan turned her in his arms, seeking out the answer in her eyes. "Morgan?"

She placed one finger against his lips. "Can we talk tomorrow morning?"

He captured her finger. "And what happens tonight?"

She took a step away from him and released the sash on the robe. It fell to her feet in a fluffy pool of white. "Anything we want to."

Evan scooped her up into his arms and carried her out into the bedroom. As he laid her on the bed, he murmured against her lips, "God does still answer prayers."

As the sun rose the next morning, Evan brought their joined hands up to the light. "You have the softest skin."

Morgan smiled and kissed his shoulder. "You're biased."

"Of course, I am."

Silence fell for the space of a heartbeat. Then, Morgan asked, "Evan?"

"Yeah?"

"Did you really want to get divorced?"

"Never. I think things just got so tough for us. You couldn't handle my job and I couldn't handle your desire to make something out of your legal career. Now, I see we could have compromised."

More silence fell until Morgan offered, "Do you think we could compromise now?"

Evan lowered their hands and turned his head on the pillow to see her face. "Morgan, what are you asking?"

She cleared her throat and smiled into his sleepy eyes. "I don't want to go back to Raleigh. I want to stay here with you. I know I might be assuming a lot, but I think we should start over, maybe not pick up where we left off, but maybe there's another chance for us. Maybe..." Her words were silenced by Evan's kiss. Her eyes widened for a brief moment and then she fell into the bliss for a long moment. When Evan finally lifted his head, her face was flushed, her lips swollen.

"I'll take that as an agreement," she whispered.

"See? That law degree comes in handy after all," he grinned.

Morgan rolled into his arms with a smile and as her head settled against his chest, she realized, after years of trying to find her way in life, she'd finally found her way home.

About the Author

Rachel Carrington is a published author of contemporary, fantasy and paranormal romances. To learn more about Rachel, please visit www.dawnrachel.com. Send an email to Rachel at rachelcarrington@moongladeeliteauthors.com or join her Yahoo! group to join in the fun with other readers by sending a blank e-mail to:

DawnRachelCarringtonnewsletter-subscribe@yahoogroups.com.

A battle begins between Shane, who knows what he wants and Cassie who does everything she can tries to keep a distance between herself and the very handsome sheriff.
But Cassie's ex is back and he wants her dead.

Taking Chase
© *2006 Lauren Dane*

Cassie Gambol is on the run. In what seems like another lifetime, her ex-husband nearly ended her life and effectively ended her successful career as a vascular surgeon. But even though the justice system found him guilty of attempted murder, he fled while awaiting sentencing and Carly Sunderland became Cassie Gambol.

Fleeing Los Angeles, she heads to small and off the map Petal, Georgia to start her life again.

Shane Chase, a man who's held himself away from commitment since his fiancée dumped him several years before knows the beautiful newcomer is hiding something. He's wildly attracted to her strength and her underlying vulnerability as well.

But the last thing Cassie wants is another big, overwhelming man who wants to control her life. A battle begins between Shane, who knows what he wants and Cassie, who knows she needs to do everything she can to keep a distance between herself and the very handsome sheriff.

But Cassie's ex is back and he wants her dead.

Book Two of the Chase Brothers

Available now in ebook and print from Samhain Publishing.

Enjoy the following excerpt from Taking Chase...

"I'm gonna kiss you now, Cassie Gambol."

"Why? I mean, why do you want me? I don't understand it. I can't lie and tell you I don't know you've been regarded as a player here in Petal. I like men, yes, but I'm afraid of being a casual indulgence to a man like you."

"There's not a damned thing about the way I feel about you that's casual. Now, I've been dying to do this for so long." He closed the last bit of distance between them and he brushed his mouth over hers. His lips were lush and delicious, spicy and masculine, just like the rest of him. They both groaned as he moved away.

"Cassie, you fascinate me. I'm shocked by how much I want you. I think I started wanting you when you kicked my ass at pool. No, I'm a damned liar. Since you stumbled out of your wrecked car and called my momma Crash." He put his face into her neck and inhaled deeply. "God, you smell good."

"Shampoo, sweat and a little bit of Delice," she breathed out, running her tongue over the lips he'd just touched with his own. A sense of unreality washed over her. The connection between them was warm and sticky. Lethargic with want, she let him hold her against his body. The heat of him blanketed her skin. Her nipples hardened against the wall of his chest and a libido that she'd thought beaten out of her roared back to life. There was a moment where she wondered if she was dreaming. Hell, if it wasn't she sure didn't want to wake up.

"Mmm." He licked his lips as she'd just done and a shiver ran through her. "You taste good, too. Better than you should. I ought to be running out the door but damned if you don't make me want things I'd thought I'd never want with a woman again."

His hand rested at the small of her back, hot and inescapably present. The other rested on her shoulder. He held her in his orbit physically and mentally. His presence was so intense it boggled her mind. Things tightened low in her gut as her skin tingled everywhere he touched her. And yet, aside from general nervousness, she wasn't afraid.

She caught her lip in her teeth and he groaned softly. "I know you want me too." Leaning in, he pressed a hot, wet kiss to the hollow just below her ear. "I can feel your nipples against my chest," he murmured, breath stirring the wisps of hair around her ear. His tongue darted inside and then he caught the lobe between his teeth. She shivered, going weak in the knees. "But I want more than your physical need of me. Let's have dinner. Some snuggling on your couch. A liberal smattering of smooches. Let me get to know you as a woman."

"I...yes." She nodded, incapable of further speech. Especially when his grin widened and he looked like a predator.

They sat down and began to dish up the food, digging in. He watched her and she laughed. "What? Do I have a bean spout between my teeth?"

"No," he chuckled. "I just like the way you look here with me." He shrugged. "And I like that you eat. Not like some dainty thing who wants everyone to believe she survives on air and mist, but you eat like a real person."

"Is that your finessed way of telling me I eat like a pig?"

He threw his head back and laughed. "Oh the unwinnable guy question. Darlin' you do not eat like a pig. You eat like a human who likes to eat. I *like* that."

She narrowed her eyes at him for a moment and shrugged before going back to her plate. She'd only just put the weight on she lost from the hospital and afterwards in the last three months or so.

They kept a wide berth around what happened the night before but Cassie was pretty sure Maggie had told him about Terry. He didn't seem freaked, which made her more comfortable.

After they'd eaten, he helped her clean up and get the dishes in the dishwasher before they retired to the couch.

"Let's get comfortable here, shall we, darlin'? Because I have some serious smooching planned and we should do it right." He winked and pulled her into his lap, her body straddling his.

The hard ridge of his cock fit up against her and she undulated, grinding herself over him without even thinking of it. Little flares of pleasure played up her spine and the muscles inside her pussy fluttered and contracted.

One of his eyebrows rose slowly and his hands slid to rest at her waist. "So that's how it's gonna be, huh? Mmm. You feel so damned good, Cassie. I need to kiss you again." Arching his neck up, he brought his lips to hers with crushing intensity.

Her head swam as she drowned in him. In a myriad of ways he affected her, overwhelmed her, turned her on and turned her out. Helpless to do anything more than hang on, she slid her hands up his chest and neck and into his hair. The soft, cool silk of it flowed over her skin, his skull solid and sure beneath her palms.

Grunting in satisfaction, he slanted his mouth to get more of her. His tongue slipped in between her teeth and he tasted her, met her warmth with his own. Her elemental flavor rocked him, he couldn't get enough. When she sucked at his tongue, he pulled her to him tighter and delighted in the moan that came from her lips. Swallowed it down with the rest of her that he took from the kiss.

God he wanted more. The luscious flesh of her bottom lip seduced him as he sucked it into his mouth. Arching into him with a breathy sigh, she traced the outline of his upper lip with the tip of her tongue. Down over the seam of his mouth where her lip was captured, the wetness of her tongue, the tentative and yet utterly carnal way she responded, drew him in.

It'd never been like this with a woman before. Intense, sure. Really good, that too. But so good, so right that it made his chest ache with want and need of *this* woman in his arms? Never.

Damn, he was falling for Cassie. Scratch that—had *fallen* for Cassie and he wasn't running. No, he wanted more. Wanted to gorge himself on every drop of her he could get as long as he could get it. He wanted to see what kind of tomorrow he could build with this woman. Cassie Gambol wasn't a casual indulgence at all, she was big league addiction and instead of fear, there was only joy that he'd found it at last.

It took every bit of his self control to keep his hands resting at her waist instead of sliding down to cup her ass. She was so soft against him, so warm and pliant—everything sexy and earthy, he wanted to take her in the grass under the moon, the dew on his naked skin as he watched her in the silvery light. She was a goddess come alive in his arms.

Discover the Talons Series

5 STEAMY NEW PARANORMAL ROMANCES
TO HOOK YOU IN

Kiss Me Deadly, by Shannon Stacey
King of Prey, by Mandy M. Roth
Firebird, by Jaycee Clark
Caged Desire, by Sydney Somers
Seize the Hunter, by Michelle M. Pillow

AVAILABLE IN EBOOK—COMING SOON IN PRINT!

WWW.SAMHAINPUBLISHING.COM

GET IT NOW

GREAT cheap FUN

Discover eBooks!
THE FASTEST WAY TO GET THE HOTTEST NAMES

Get your favorite authors on your favorite reader, long before they're out in print! Ebooks from Samhain go wherever you go, and work with whatever you carry—Palm, PDF, Mobi, and more.

Samhain
publishing, ltd.

WWW.SAMHAINPUBLISHING.COM

Printed in the United States
74465LV00004B/133-411